Andrea

M000222833

Thank-you friend! Writing
and Publishing Silverfish was a long
road, but I took it One-Day-At-A-Time!

Love,

Silverfish

Silverfish

Hobie Anthony

WHISKEY TIT
NYC & VT

This is a work of fiction. Names, characters, places, and incidents either
are the product of the author's imagination or are used fictitiously.
 Though there are blanks that might be filled in by the reader,
 resemblance to actual persons, living or dead, events, or locales is
entirely coincidental.

Published in the United States by Whisk(e)y Tit: www.whiskeytit.com. If
you wish to use or reproduce all or part of this book for any means, please
let the author and publisher know. You're pretty much required to,
legally.

Cover art by Jonathan Treadway. Find him on Instagram
@jonathantreadwayartist.

ISBN 978-0999621578

First Whisk(e)y Tit paperback edition.

Contents

1

Silverfish

In this place, wires run everywhere. They're attached to the walls with plastic fasteners, tied to water pipes, crammed into windowsills. They tangle and run like snakes chasing a mouse. If I watch them long enough, I see them writhe. When I sleep or hold my eyes closed long enough, they move and multiply. Here, in the corner, there used to be five wires running down to the floor, now there are fifteen wires stretching to the far corner along the ceiling. I note the changes in my book.

I am the caretaker of this place. I take care of LaMore, he runs things. I owe everything to LaMore. He has given all of this to me and I do what he needs. I run his errands. I take care of things he does not want to do. I cannot leave. I do not wish to leave. This is my home, my place to protect and serve. I keep it running but LaMore is the king. He's huge and strong and carries razor-sharp knives.

I am known by what I do. I am called Caretaker. I assemble rats to help me find my true name. They are smart and I know how to hear what they are saying. I have a method and I will create the device. I look for only the smartest ones, the rats who will like me and serve me.

I do not know where I came from. I have a room in the basement. The room is large and I have a bed, a sofa, and a rug. There are windows and a door in this room. Behind, there are dark rooms, hallways which go forever into the dark. I found a bathroom there. I never bring a light when I go. There are more than spirits there, there are creatures in the dark rooms who do not like light. I hear them scurry around, watching me, and I leave food for them to find. I clean up the rat carcasses they leave behind.

I clean. When the silverfish come out, I clean them up with a broom and pan as they crawl across the carpet, wormy in their new life. Some hide and grow to spiny, hairy adults, slipping across the floor, hiding between my stomping treads. I can never catch up. They seem to disappear at the times when LaMore receives raw materials from the pale men in dark suits, but come back even stronger. There are never silverfish upstairs, only people, and LaMore. The people never eat, so there is never puke or shit to clean, only sweat from fucking and the dust that accumulates with time.

I read and talk to the rats. It's not safe enough upstairs to stay for long. The air is poison when they cook the drugs and the men are dangerous, especially LaMore, he's the only one who's always here. I told him he should use a room back in the dark to cook, but he says no, we cannot do that. That is the only time I've seen LaMore scared.

Knives and guns and money keep things moving. The women come and go. I hear women upstairs now, screaming in pleasure. It could be pain. They scream and scream, sometimes for hours. Sometimes several scream at once. They howl and carry on, like dogs barking in the night. I sit still and listen, the rats listen. The men grunt and growl. Silence.

I cut the wires; I strip them, expose copper which shines and gives me hope. The wires conduct and transmit. I twist them together. They will work.

Every day I wake at dawn and walk through the woods to the market. I buy food for the day, enough for two meals, two scoops of rice, a piece of fruit, a bag of vegetables. LaMore gave me a hotplate. The water runs clear after a minute or two.

A simple, harmless trap catches the rats. They can't resist the cupcakes I find behind the grocery store. I put them in cages I make from strong screen stapled to scrap wood. LaMore gave me a small rifle to shoot them with, but I would rather trap them. The rats are smart; they are smarter than me. I keep them alive and they keep me company. They are almost ready. They will help me.

I feed them. One screeches at me. I see hatred in his eyes and hollow soul. It gives me chills, he would throw me out, he would let me die alone and in the rain. I never let him starve. He turns on me with hate. If they do not like me we cannot continue. I put him in the dark rooms. I do not feed him, maybe he will be eaten by the things living there.

I go upstairs and tell the men what I have done; they nod and look at me. They lie naked with girls on the floor. They roll over and fuck. The women come to buy drugs. They arrive with healthy teeth, full rumps. They laugh and party. Some of them make movies for LaMore in the back bedroom and sometimes down here, in the dark rooms. LaMore hates it back there. It scares him. I stand in when the other guy's dick goes soft from drugs or overuse. I make extra money this way. I make myself pure after, cleaning more and more, inside and out.

The girls stay for weeks or months, until they slip out the door with their clothes hanging off of them, shoulders gone skeletal, hollow eyes, and black teeth. They all seem the same, moving through. Some fight with each other, over who is prettiest or whose man is whose. The men laugh and scratch their bony ribs.

This is not the place where I was born. LaMore assures me of this. I woke up here one morning. From nowhere, knowing nothing. I felt the cool, hard floor on my back and opened my eyes.

A shotgun.

My forehead.

I said why not. I said if not you then someone else; if not someone else then I'll have to do it myself. So do it, I said. LaMore put the shotgun in my mouth. His face half-scarred by fire, half pocked with acne; gold teeth; left arm cloaked in a black glove. There's something funny about you. He pushed a long lock of black hair from his face. I want to kill you, he said, but I like pets and you look like a good one. He propped the shotgun on his shoulder, locked his eyes to mine.

His gloved hand reached out and covered my face. It smelled of fresh rubber, it pulled my skin. The fingers moved independently in circles on my forehead and face, clamping pressure on my skull, massaging bone. I heard a hum deep in my brain. Looking into his eyes, I saw something unseen and felt something ineffable that struck terror and awe in my soul. We became bonded in that moment, brothers. I have no name, but I do have a brother, I thought. He pushed my head back and laughed and said, I'll make you a deal.

He made me caretaker of rats and silverfish and wires. He spared my life and gave me a job. LaMore gives me money for food and I always have plenty left over. He tells me to buy beer or pornographic magazines, but I keep the extra money in a box under my bed.

LaMore calls down the stairs. Yo, Caretaker, got a package. I don't like to leave. Things disappear when you leave them. Caretaker, come up and take this across town. I have to keep my rats, they're too important. I don't want to go, I have to catch rats, I say. You better go, if you know what's good for you. He has a knife; he tosses a backpack down to me. We'll be here when you get back, and you better come back, caretaker.

It's raining. It's cool and gray. I pick a bike to ride from the pile of abandoned cycles in the garage. I find an old mountain bike which fits me. It's a long ride. The rain needles my face on the down-hills. My clothes saturate. The package is safe, it is wrapped in layers of tape and paper and the bag is waterproof, too.

The house is like LaMore's. Weeds growing in driveway cracks. Old bicycles rusting in the backyard. There are new people at this house. I've been here before, but I don't recognize any of them. A man, who looks like LaMore but shorter, asks me am I the guy; I say yes, I'm the guy. I have the package. He asks why

I'm all wet but he laughs and I don't have a chance to answer. The other guy never laughed like that. I open the bag and give them the package and they give me one in return.

They ask me to smoke a joint and watch television. My house no longer has a television. LaMore threw a chair through the last one and there is a scorch mark from the fire. Here, wires run from ceiling to floor, spaced every few feet along the wall. They are the same sort of wires I have. The more of the joint I smoke, the more the wires move. The same sort of girls are here, too, thin and wearing few, if any, clothes. They are all pretty until you see them.

The pot relaxes me. The messages on television pound my body, pulling me one way then the next. There are too many messages and it's hard to keep track. The girl next to me holds a remote control and giggles. Characters scream at one another in a courtroom. The judge screams back. There is a war on another channel. Heavy dramatic music thrums as the camera shows a woman's eyes in close-up. Children scream with glee at breakfast cereal. All of the characters' skin looks like they have no pores and no sweat.

The girl next to me lights another joint and blows smoke into my mouth; she puts a needle into her foot. She pushes back into the sofa cushion and gives a growling moan. The remote control falls onto the floor. She moves like a cat, or a snake. She crouches over my lap. She unzips my pants, pushes them down, sucks my dick into her mouth. I come during a soap commercial.

I pick out a different bike, a fast, black 10-speed. Everyone gathers to say goodbye, to watch someone leave. A woman with graying hair and a twitch in her face puts a helmet on my head. You'll be safer, she says, the helmet will make you safe and sound and you can come back sometime – you like the girls? You like me? She makes me feel ill. She fastens the strap beneath my chin, adjusts it on my head. The rain has stopped and the air is fresh. I leave the helmet under a bush two blocks away.

The house is there when I return, but things are different. A man is on his knees in the front yard, clipping grass with hedge clippers; a woman cleans the windows with a hand rag and a cup of water. A man takes two sweeps with a broom, then dusts off the broom, then sweeps again. He crouches to inspect the corner of the carport which he is working on. He sweeps it again. He looks at me and says, you should never ask about where it comes from; take it, take it, enjoy the high, never ask questions.

LaMore is at the sink. He's washing his knife. He's wearing a tank-top shirt and I see where his black glove meets his shoulder. When he moves, I see bumpy, hairless skin underneath. He asks me if I have the mother-fucking package and points the knife at my chest. I see blood in the hilt, blood spatter caked in his scar. I give him the bag. He asks me what took so long. I say we watched television. We smoke a joint. He holds the knife to my throat and tells me that if I was going to be late, I should have called. He slides the tip under my chin. He makes me look at the ceiling. With a flick, he cuts me. He laughs. A mouth full of gold and silver teeth. I feel the blood pour down my neck, dribble on to my chest. Caretaker, I like you, you keep your goddamn mouth shut, he says.

I clean my chin in the bathroom. He cut me to the bone. A man is in the bathtub bleeding from his belly. He moans. He asks my name. The question I can never answer. My name. I don't remember, or the word does not come to mind fast enough, it evaporates on its way to the air. I stop looking for the word. The rats will help me find my name. I bandage my chin. Gurgles and spittle-sputters echo off the tile in the bathroom. His eyes freeze. I close the door on my way out.

There is a lump in my bed. A body. I pad my way over, silent. It is a girl, a redheaded girl. I think I've seen her. There are so many and they all seem the same. She is sleeping. I've never seen anyone sleep here. So silent and peaceful. Nothing is peaceful here, there is always a scream or blood or brutal violence waiting to happen. It's important to be alert here, even when I sleep. But, here, in my bed, is the perfect picture of peace. She looks like she might be pretty, too. Her face is skeletal, but something is there, a structure that can hold a fleshy beauty. If I even knew what that was.

LaMore calls down. Caretaker, you have a job to do, get your ass up here.

The man in the bathroom has died. He lies there with his eyes open, blood drying in his mouth. We put a hook in the ceiling and string him up by his feet. The body hangs like a pig in a slaughterhouse. LaMore cuts his throat to drain the blood and scalds the body with shower-water. LaMore smokes cigarettes. The sun sets as the last of the blood dribbles out. In a locked closet in the back bedroom, I find a bag large enough for the man.

He's dope-fiend skinny. He fits in the bag. We carry him to a old, shiny-black sedan in the driveway. It's like what the men in dark suits drive. We'll put him in the trunk, LaMore says, you drive.

LaMore directs me out through country roads. The route becomes gray with mist as we approach the large mountain. I turn on the headlights. The car is large and powerful, LaMore makes me go fast. I put on my seat-belt, but LaMore slices it off. Pussies wear seatbelts, he says, go faster. I know you ain't no pussy. No sir, you're a genuine badass, Mr. Caretaker. That's why I keep you around. You seem all quiet and harmless, but I know better. I've seen it down in you that first day I found you, that's why I kept you. You'll come through at a moment's notice. You don't care at all, no sir, you don't give a shit; a stone-cold killer if you need to be. I saw how you strung that guy up, like he was meat. Hell, you even left him to die in there. You took care of your chin and you left his sorry motherfucking ass for dead.

He's just another addict, I say. You stabbed him, so he must've fucked up. I figure why mess with something that's done. Nothing I could do.

The road gets curvy and dark. The mist is now thick fog. We rise in elevation. My ears pop. LaMore tells me to go faster. I accelerate. The car handles the mountain curves. The body rolls and rumbles in the trunk.

LaMore says to turn off where the trees part and there seems to be no road. We drive over weeds, shrubs, and laurel then there is a road headlight-high in weeds. The large car is sure-footed. Large, mossy trees line the road. We bump over roots. There are no fresh tracks. Raccoons glare glowing eyes and scamper away.

We come to a clearing and there is a large mansion built in some old style of architecture. I pull the car up to the front door and we unload the body. Staircases go up to either side as we enter the large double doors. Each set of stairs is matched by a set descending to a basement. Men in dark suits and pale skin walk around in silence. LaMore does not speak to them. The room is cavernous: five fireplaces blaze, two on each side and one at the end of the room. The men gather in small groups. Individuals peel off, join other groups, and are replaced.

We carry the body toward the large fireplace at the end of the massive hall. I carry the torso. I walk backwards, facing LaMore. His eyes are locked on me. I keep my eyes on him. I am sure that I'm not about to hit anything. LaMore watches out— he does not allow bumbling. We reach the fireplace. It could hold ten more junkies like this guy. LaMore and I swing the body and release it to the pyre. The black bag melts and burns away; the man's blood-stained clothes and body lie exposed. Skin burns and sizzles. His juices cook out; he burns to a crisp. We watch the flesh burn away, leaving only a skeleton in the fire. Caretaker, it is your time, LaMore says.

My arms are bound behind me. A bag goes over my head. A needle pierces my butt. I feel dizzy. My face feels warm and wet. I collapse.

I hear movement around me. I open my eyes. The pale men are arranged around me in a semi-circle. I am tied to a rack. My arms and legs are open to a vee. I am naked. The cut on my chin has reopened and is dripping blood down my chest. LaMore is nowhere to be seen.

One of the men approaches me. He speaks to me but I hear him inside my brain, not with my ears. His lipless mouth moves but the words don't match. You are brought to us so we may see how you are to us. You are part of what we are; you will become one of us and today is the first part of what must be done. My muscles tense. My eyes close. I don't know if my body is acting on its own or if it's being controlled by the men.

I sense the crowd closing in on me. I hear many voices, but no words. It's the buzzing sound of a million bees in my head at once. I want to block it out, but there is no way to resist. They are in my brain, they have complete control of my body. Something sucks my chin, drinks my blood. Something like snakes slither around my ankles, wrists, then arms, legs. In a few moments I'm covered. Smaller things enter my ears, nose, mouth. The noise in my mind is full-volume and I want to scream, but my mouth is full. My eyes open, involuntarily. I cannot blink. Their arms are long, bumpy, green tentacles, probing my body. At the top of the semi-circle, directly in front of me, the men part and the largest of them all comes through. His legs do not move as he approaches me. He holds his arms out and they morph into tentacles. His mouth moves, I will see for myself if this is what I want. If what LaMore has said is true, you will become part of us.

His tentacles move up under me and penetrate me. My mind turns inside-out. I close my eyes to see kaleidoscopic colors and patterns. Are you what we want? I want to shit, puke, pee. My eyes are popping out of my head. Tears stream down my face. The buzzing, the buzzing. The pressure builds in my head, like it might explode. I scream, the buzzing shreds my mind. Louder. More pressure. Louder.

I am going to die.

I am going to die.

I am going to die

Black.

Morning.

I wake in a chair on the carport. Some guy rifles through my pockets, but there's nothing there. I smack his head. He yelps in fright and runs away. I want to forget what happened. I hear an echo of the buzzing. It will never go away.

◇

In my basement room, I turn on the radio. The girl is in my bed. The rats like the jazz station. I assemble their cages in a circle and I talk to them. I tell them how the world is a good place. I tell them about rain and bicycles and how riding downhill is like flying. My ass and insides feel raw and alien. I want to puke. I feed the rats oats and tell them about the blowjob. They like this story. I try to focus on the blowjob.

The lump moves. She pokes her head out from under the covers. I've seen her upstairs. She is thin, her hair is fire-red, and her eyes look like sockets with dots of coal in the middle. She wants to know who I was talking to. I tell her.

She wants to know if she can stay here. I say why not upstairs. She shakes her head; she says too much screaming; she says too much blood. I need to sleep, she says, please let me sleep. She rolls over to face the wall. I ask her if she wants some food, rice and vegetables. I make as much as I have. She tries. She mouths the food, swallows some rice. She sleeps. I eat the food.

I have a sofa to lay on and a lamp to read my books by. I read what I find on sidewalks around town. I don't remember what they are about, but I see the characters. I never know their names. I remember what they look like, how they smell. I feel them around me. Spacemen, housewives, government spies and reckless drunks all live in my mind, keeping me company.

Scream.

I sit up straight in the dark.

She screams, Let me go, let me go, let me go.

The girl screamed but now is silent, balled up under the covers. I hover over her. Breath moves the sheet in moonlight. She's kicked the covers from her bony body. She's lying stiff and rigid. I pull the sheet and blanket over her.

There are people in the market this morning. It's usually empty. People block the produce. I don't want to get close, to feel their vibrations; they all seem to hum. Look at me, turn away. My rice, vegetables, fruit, and extra. Extra. My basket is heavier. The check-out man picks up the carton of juice and asks is it mine. I nod at him. Bread, too? He looks at me and puts it in the bag.

LaMore is in the backyard, staring up into the trees. He wants to know the day, date, and time. I tell him. He paces back and forth. His eyes are gone wild from too much speed. He asks me again and I tell him. The men in the trees disappear in the sunlight, he says, they're all chickenshit bastards who won't face me in the day.

What's in the bag? He says, you got more than normal. What are you feeding those rats? A girl came down, I say. Which one? The one with red hair. He pulls his knife from its sheath. If you let her go, you'll be like the guy yesterday and all those rats and silverfish and the raccoon he saw on the street the other day that looked like a furry manhole cover. You're the goddamn caretaker so you better goddamn take care of that girl. Kill her. She's okay, I say; she seems sick; she doesn't want to run; she wanted a bed. You should fuck her, wear her ass out. Then, when she starts talking too much, I'll give you a knife. I have a perfect one with a hand-carved handle made from a bear's bone. I've never used it. I'll get it ready special for her, extra-sharp. By the time she feels it, it'll already be done.

I look at the bed. The girl is watching me. I see her eyes blinking in the shadow of her sockets. I offer food. She nods and props up. I hand her the carton of juice, but she is too weak to handle it. I pour it into her mouth and some spills on the bed. It turns her lips red. I see the bones in her chest. I can see that her eyes have color, dark. Her breasts are withered cylinders. I ask her how long and she doesn't know. I tear off a piece of bread and place it in her mouth. I pour the juice in her mouth. She coughs. She lies back. I need my sleep, she says, I need to sleep forever.

I have five rats who like me. They listen to my stories. I think it is time for our experiment. I have wire cutters and strippers. I took wires from the walls. The rats watch, curious. I feed them more oats and tell them, soon. I strip the wires to the bare copper, to the shiny inside. I twist the wire into three little ropes of five wires each. I braid them into a single, beautiful, rope. This is how I dreamt it. I know this is right.

I make special copper fasteners which extend down into the cages to pick up vibrations from the rats. I run the rope through the fasteners creating a circuit through all of the cages. It is ready.

I prepare myself. I drink a quart of saltwater, mixed in a perfect solution, and lie down. The water won't be absorbed, it's the same weight as blood, and it will flush impurities. When the water runs its course, when my body is purified, I can begin. The salt makes me a better conductor. Purity makes me a better receptor.

After an hour, my abdomen gurgles and I clinch up. I feel my way through the dark rooms to find the toilet. Bodies lurk around me in the dark. I smell warm breath. I hear hissed whispers; I can't tell if they're in my head or in my ears. Nothing makes any sense, no words come through. They don't touch me. I sense them before we collide. They lead me, they block my way, they ensure I go the fastest way.

I make it just in time. My bowel explodes into the toilet, a gush of fluid. It doesn't stop. I sit in the dark as my body convulses and purges the poisons it holds. With each lurch of my abdomen, a red field appears before me. Finally, I am clean. I am clean and shiny like copper wire. I am ready.

The girl is moves, murmurs, dreams. The rats nibble at the rest of their oats. I sit in the circle with them. I sit upright on my butt bones. My insides feel clean, empty. I pick up the ends of the copper rope. I close my eyes. I breathe and empty my mind. Images of the rats come. Images of the girl. I breathe in and out slowly. Thoughts of the grocery store creep in. Thoughts of the blowjob. Breathe. Empty. Thoughts of LaMore. Breathe, Empty, Breathe, Breathe…

I open my eyes. The rats are still here, the room is still here. The girl looks at me. She has propped her head on a second pillow. What are you doing? I am talking to the rats; they are very smart. They teach me things. What do you want to know, she says. I want to know my name. Why don't you pick your own name, I can help you; I know a lot of names.

I ask if she wants food. I cook the vegetables soft, making mushy rice. She can't give me a name, that's a job for the rats, not her. She can't handle much food. I give her more water and juice.

She tells me about where she is from, how she got here. She is from Seattle, about four hours away, she says. She ran away from her father. Her mother left them a few years ago. He was not bad; he was never home. He was working. I left him before he came home from work. I left in the middle of the day on a Monday. Her chin drops and I feel her sadness move through me.

She keeps talking and I let her. I watch her eyes, her mouth. She speaks soft and gentle, yet strong. Her voice is like nimble fingers on my muscles and in my throat. Not like the brittle ramble of the girls upstairs.

I tell her to sleep. She can't want it if she's asleep. Tell it you don't want it anymore, ask it to go away. Tell it thanks but no thanks. She looks at me and I see a person behind the eyes. I look and look. I feel a warmth in her that is reaching out to me. My face sags a bit where

I didn't know it was tight. She asks me to lie down with her and I do.

She stays with me and I feed her. I keep notes of her eating and sleeping. She eats a little more as time goes on. She sleeps less each day. LaMore sends me on errands and she is still here when I return, alive. She reads my books and wants more. LaMore looks at me funny when I come upstairs now, says things are really quiet downstairs, what the hell are y'all doing? What do y'all talk about? Why aren't you fucking her? I tell him nothing and I run his errands. I ride through the city streets as fast as the bicycle will carry me. I find small piles of books on the sidewalks. I carry home what I think she'll like. The books with the flashy covers I leave behind, the more serious-looking ones I bring to her. She reads them and likes them. I am pleased to watch her holding them.

Her cheekbones soften and her shoulders round. I have to buy twice as much food. She starts to bleed on her cycle so I have to buy that stuff, too.

One day, she tells me her name. Her name is Olwyn. I feel something deep in my loins when she says it, a warmth. Olwyn. It's a magical name, I say. I can't say anything else, but I repeat the name over and over in my head.

The rats still have not found my name. I sit with the copper rope every day, waiting, empty, silent. Olwyn says the copper is pretty, it has patina. The silverfish come back. Olwyn reads and I sit with the rats. Her eyes catch the light. The are emeralds. She plays the jazz radio station and hums syncopated riffs, creates her own solos.

Olwyn wants to leave or at least go to the store with me, but I know LaMore will kill both of us if we do that. He offers me knives whenever I see him and asks me when I'm going to be sick of her and want to get rid of her. He says she better not leave the house until she's dead. I say, you let other girls leave, why not her. He says she's different, she knows stuff. She's not normal he says.

I tell her she can't leave. I tell her LaMore will kill her if she does. She says she knows but needs to see her mother and father some time. She wants to do things and can't stay here forever. I ask her what happened. Why does LaMore want to kill her and not the other girls who leave?

She tells me the story: "I'd been tweakin' hard for a while. Maybe three days, I'm not sure. That shit was so good. But, anyway, I wanted to come down a bit; my body was giving out. I guess I was talking about it aloud, I wasn't sure what was in my head and what I was really saying. I must have said something about coming down because LaMore popped into my face and said that he could take care of that. He said to hang on and he'd take care of me. Then these strange looking dudes appeared in dark suits all with this waxy, pale skin and LaMore asked me if I wanted to come down still and I said yeah. So, he popped a spike in my leg and I kinda mellowed out. Then he gave me another. It took a while, but I guess I passed out.

"So, the next thing I know, I'm hearing voices murmuring or buzzing. It wasn't like real language, just a bunch of sounds buzzing up and down the sounds wrapped around each other. That's the only way I can describe it. It was like music but not musical really. Or some foreign music like when you listen to Asian music and it sounds funky.

"I don't know. I was laying on a bed, restrained at the wrists and ankles and I could tell I was naked. I was always naked anyway. I was numb from whatever LaMore shot me up with, but I felt something crawl up my inner thigh, like a worm or snake or something. It went in me and was wriggling all around. The buzzing got louder and more active. I could tell there were several voices buzzing. Another thing crawled up my thigh and went in, too. They kept moving like I've never felt before. I, well, I couldn't help it, man."

She looks at me with tears hanging on her eyelids, watery pools of green. I hold her and sobs wet my shirt. She trembles in my arms. She says she didn't want it to happen, she wishes she'd never left her father and Seattle. I make her tea and she holds the cup in her hands like it was liquid gold. I put my arm around her and she drinks the tea, breathing deep, shuddering. She rests her head on my shoulder. I ask her to finish her story, maybe that will help.

"It was wriggling in me and, well, it felt good. I knew I was supposed to be out cold, but I was awake and I had a feeling of ecstasy. I couldn't help myself. I started to moan and move like I was with the best lover

I'd ever had. I couldn't help it. I was not in control, I tell you. I felt violated, raped. It felt good. I didn't want those foreign things in me. All the way in me, to parts I don't think I've ever felt, it was more than sex, it was an examination.

"The buzzing increased with my moans and I cracked open my eyes. I saw these men, the pale men in the dark suits, their hands had turned into these tentacle-looking things and they were in me. All of them were in me. They had taken off their sunglasses and their eyes were these big black marbles. I was stunned and panicked but in a state of ecstasy and my body was writhing with their tentacles.

"LaMore was in the corner and he stood up and filled his syringe again. He said I needed to forget what I saw; he says I should never have woken up. He said I must had a liver like a champion. I clamped my eyes and fought the fear and bliss until the needle pricked and the world went black again. The last thing I remember is LaMore telling me I could never leave this house without him. If I did, I'd be dead.

"After that, I smoked more shit than I've ever smoked. I drank, too, and I don't like alcohol. I wanted more because every time I started coming down I felt those things in me and the more I felt them the less the feeling was good, the worse I felt.

"LaMore was always staring at me, giving me one of his looks, especially when he'd bring out one of his knives. He'd stare at me and sharpen the blade with those slow and deliberate strokes. You know that look, you see that scar even more and his muscles are bigger, that black glove seems to pulse. He told me to not even think about leaving. He said if I left I'd regret it, that there was no place for me to run that they couldn't find me. I guess he still won't let me leave I guess I know something he doesn't want me to tell – but I don't even care what those guys are or where they come from. If they've got some plan to take over the world or whatever I don't even care. They'll do it with or without me. I just want to hang out with you, leave here, find my mom or go home to my father.

"But, anyway, I had to do something. I was fed up with living like an animal. I didn't care what anyone thought, or if LaMore was going to kill me or not. Lots of other girls have committed suicide by their own hand. I figured if I was going to bring on my death, I'd do it searching out life. So, that one day, LaMore and some guy got into a fight and there was an opportunity to leave. I grabbed some stuff, but I was drugged and confused. By the time I got to the bottom of the stairs, I thought I was somewhere or someone else already and then you found me."

It wasn't hard, you were in my bed, I say to her. She wants to get in the bed now, I can tell. I know what she wants without hearing the words. She wipes her face and dries her hand on my shirt. Her eyes close and her mouth purses. I move my face closer and I can feel her exhale, smell sweetness on her breath. Our lips meet. They meet again and our mouths open; a memory comes back to my body. My mouth remembers and takes over where my brain is struck dumb. I want to take a bite of her, but I don't. I am hungry, but not fed.

Her body feels hot to the touch. Her breasts are full in my hand. She kisses my neck and my body is shot-through with electricity. I can pick her up, so I do. I carry her to the bed and lay her down. I lie next to her and our clothes fall to the floor, panties tossed off the foot of the bed. Her body is warm and electric. I roll on top of and lose myself in her.

The rain falls through the trees and it makes me happy. Olwyn lies in my bed, satisfied, and that makes me happy. The whoosh of the automatic door at the store makes me happy. That's the best word I can find for this feeling in this moment. Like a veil has been taken from between me and the rest of the world, everything is new. The store is brighter and the produce fresher. The checkout man smiles at me. I smile back at him, but look away.

I can tell that she's changed me. I know LaMore knew this. This is what he meant. She influences me, she messes with my mind. I didn't realize something so sweet and beautiful could be so poisonous. This is why the men upstairs don't talk to the girls, so the girls won't mess them up.

I come through to the other side of the woods and I see LaMore is standing on the back porch, smoking. He's pacing, looking at a knife. He looks at it, then rubs it on his gloved arm. His bushy black hair sucks in the sunlight, a black halo around his gnarled face.

He calls down to me. You gotta take a package today. I tell him okay. You still got that bitch down there? Yes. You gotta do something with her, she's a liability; you don't, I will. Yeah, I know, I know. I'm ready for one of those knives, I say to him, looking up into his face, his mouth full of metal. That's my boy, he says, you're doing fine.

Olwyn and I eat. We're quiet. We sit close. We are in each other's space. I don't touch her. I feel her and I sense her breath, her heartbeat. The food is good and I feel my body getting stronger with each bite. I have to forget what Olwyn is doing to me; I think about the knife LaMore will give me. The long razor-sharp blade, the carved handle. I think about what I will do with it. I think about what I really want to do with it. Olwyn's hand shakes and spills juice on my white t-shirt.

It's the same as a thousand times before. LaMore gives me the package. Tells me which house to deliver to. He issues threats. He paces and threatens some more. He sees me look at the knife on his belt. He tells me he's got one special for me when I return.

The streets are wet and cool. The cars are silver, white, black. Gray. The grass is green; the fir trees draw me deep into their depths. All of my muscles come to life and I pump the pedals to the top of a steep hill; a steel spring in my gut powers my movements and I am one with the simple machine. I have a mission now.

I deliver the package. They want me to smoke a joint with them. They laugh that I won't do harder stuff, that I'm scared. It's the usual routine and I appreciate the ritual. Something happened last night. It is all new. But it's not new and I know that. I'm in some delusion. I smoke the joint and watch television with them.

One of the girls, the usual girl with the cold, wet mouth, reaches for my pants. I welcome her. She has fewer teeth this week. I am thinking of Olwyn and I see this wasted creature in her place. She is what Olwyn used to be, I see the difference. Olwyn should have stayed like this: a simple creature; doomed, uncomplicated.

On the way home, I find a book of poetry on the sidewalk and a woman's shirt that Olwyn might like. I can see her wearing the shirt and reading the book, the green stripe matches her eyes. I feel a warming in my chest. I don't need this or any of this. She will never read this book, nor wear the shirt. I need to do my duty. I need to be true to the life I have, no matter who I really am or where I might be from or what my name is. This is my home and I must take care of it. Like LaMore says, she is a liability. Danger. She knows too much about the men , too much for her own good. She does not understand and her ignorance will hurt us all.

I leave the shirt and book. I keep riding. Misty rain starts to come down and I feel each tiny drop as I fly down the big hill. Each drop hits my face and I imagine them as needles poking into me; they punish me for getting so soft so fast. I think back to that first day when I found her in my bed. I should have kicked her out then. I should have taken her to LaMore so he could do what he needed to do with her. But I had to play with her. I thought she'd offer an answer like I think my rats offer me a name. I thought she could answer a question my body was asking and she did. But my heart got involved and that is not allowed. Not with her.

I remember her curled, innocent, sleeping in my

bed. I couldn't help it. She was beautiful and tragic. I didn't ask for this. I didn't offer her my bed or my care. She took them like a thief takes. She lured me with her eyes, her beautiful hair, and a voice that struck straight to my heart. I have to send her back to where she came. I have to return those emerald eyes to black.

I grind my feet into the pedals. I press for more and more speed down the hill. I look down to check the gear and make sure my pants don't get caught in the chain. I look up; a small dog is standing directly in my path. He barks. My foot slips on the pedal. I wrench the handlebars to avoid hitting the dog and fly into the other lane. A car is coming. I can't do a thing. I have no control. I lean over the handlebars, one foot clinging to a pedal, the other leg swings out for balance. The car horn blares through headlights flashing and I see the curb. My front tire slams; my head meets a chain-link fence.

It's not bad, I tell the driver. I'm okay, just a cut on the forehead, busted front wheel. She offers to give me a ride. I can walk it off. She wants to take me to a hospital. I'm fine. A ride home? I live around the corner, I tell her. She leaves.

I have LaMore's money and that's all I need. I drop the bicycle in an alley once the woman is gone. The rain soaks to my skin as I walk. Every step makes my stomach hurt more.

I don't want to do what I have to do. It has come to this. I remember her sitting in the lamplight, finishing a book before bed. Her hair seemed to glow and even in the dark her eyes gleamed emerald when she would get into bed and tell me about the story she had read. She made them all exciting and new, even the books I'd already read.

I don't know why I had to push it. Why did she tempt me so much? Ending up in bed with her, fucking her, was not what I needed. It was what I wanted and there was a difference. I'd been happy before, with my rats and my struggle against the silverfish. Now, I would have to be miserable. She'd built a space in me and I have to move her out and leave that space empty. It is the right thing. LaMore knows best. It is his house and his rule.

Where have you been? LaMore is in the kitchen, sharpening a knife. Bike wreck, I say. Your head is fucked up. You should wear a helmet. Give me the money. I give him the money and he counts it. He's pleased. Here's a good knife and something extra. He hands me a long, sheathed knife and two one-hundred dollar bills. That should do the trick, he says. Just slip it in, nice and easy, I prefer the esophagus. It won't take any effort, kid; it's like butter with a knife that sharp. I'll find you a new pig to pump in a few days. You'll forget.

I stand and look into the living room where a man is fucking a girl with speed-freak desperation. The girl's eyes are closed and her mouth is open, panting on all fours. His sweat drips onto her back. She starts to moan. My stomach is in knots. I hold the knife in my hand and unsnap the sheath, pulling out the blade. It's about a foot long and reflects my face. I tilt it to reflect her tits, rocking back and forth with deep groans. I put my thumb on the blade and slide it along the edge; a pearl of blood emerges before I feel a sting.

I open the door and make each step down slow and soft. I don't hear her; she never makes much noise. I imagine she's taking a nap or reading. I imagine her long red hair covering her face to concentrate on a book, studying a sentence.

I concentrate on the steps until I reach the floor. I turn and look into the room. She is on the sofa, asleep with a worn-out paperback on her chest. Her chest rises and falls. I remember her breasts last night. Her nipples and her whispered pleasure when I kissed them. I am taking my last look at her. Still and peaceful. The rats make noise, squealing, screeching and rattling cages. She stirs. Her eyes stay closed.

I unsheathe the knife. My bashed forehead warps in the metal mirror, the trail of blood from my thumb is dried on the blade. I sit on top of her stomach. Her eyes open and find the weapon.

LaMore?

It's the best for us.

He's not good, you know, she says.

He's what I have. He saved my life. You can't stay.

Silverfish?

Rats, too, I say. The rats are all I need.

They don't know your name.

They will.

Is this my end?

Yes. If not me, then him.

Say my name, I want you to say my name and tell

me that it's the end. Her eyes are locked on to mine. I cannot look away. You owe me that.

Olwyn.

I look at her and I cannot say another word. Frozen. The knife is heavy in my hand. Her face is still and tears stream down either side of her face, the emerald irises magnified in liquid. She doesn't sob.

Put it in, she says. Tears stream and her face curls and reddens. Put it in my chest. I want to feel it pierce my heart. That blade will do it. I won't fight you.

I slice open her shirt and expose her milky skin. I feel her ribcage with my left hand. I want the blade to slide between the bones and straight to the organs. Easy. Painless. One cut. I don't know any religious words. This is sacrifice. This is duty. I hope that is enough. We are quiet. We look at one another. I put one finger on a rib and another on the next to guide the blade.

Her chest heaves and her skin becomes gooseflesh. I feel a chill and my hair stands on end. We've been touched by something at the same time. Her eyes tell me it's true. Our bodies are communicating. Another wave. Her pupils dilate. I put the point of the blade between my fingers. It cuts the surface of her skin and blood beads, then rolls down to the fabric.

I want to tell her so many things. How I hate her for showing up and how I love her, the beauty and terror she has brought. I want to tell her everything I know, even if I cannot remember my life, even if I don't know my age. It's welling inside me, all this I must tell her. It wants to explode from me and cover her, but I only have the blade do my talking. She is still and patient. A stream of blood rolls down the side of her body. Her eyes blink, watching and waiting for me to act.

My eyes sting. I cannot move. Tears well up. My muscles go slack in my arms and shoulders. My hand drops the knife.

I cannot.

What will we do?

Tears dribble from my eyes onto her face as I lower down. My jaw won't work and my lips can barely move. I press my mouth to hers.

We have to run. Olwyn looks to the door. LaMore will see us, I say. He's looking for a body. He's waiting for me. We can't go out. We have to go in, back to the dark places. LaMore only visits there, he's afraid back there. I've seen his fear when we've made movies and when I've asked him to cook drugs there.

Olwyn doesn't like it back there. The dark is scary, she says. I tell her it's dark or death. LaMore won't just kill us, he will make us pay. I'd do it quick, LaMore makes his enemies suffer.

We have only a few items: extra clothes, a book Olwyn wants, the knife. I open the cages for the rats. They look at me, confused. I give them the food I've saved for them and they eat. Across the room, Olwyn sorts her things.

We face each other and look at each other's eyes. The green is brighter than I've seen, her hair is aflame in the window. I take a step closer and I'm enveloped in her space. I've passed into her field of energy. I wonder if she felt me, too. I step to her and our bodies are pressing. Her breath is on me. We embrace. It's not the last time; it's the first.

The darkness is total. Olwyn puts a hand on my shoulder. She carries our bag. I walk in front with hands extended. I don't sense the creatures. We meet a wall that I don't remember. Things change in the dark rooms. We turn and continue. There is no sign of light, we haven't reached an end, or returned to the beginning.

We walk and walk. I lose all sense of direction. We could be upside down, we could be on another planet. The floor declines and the air gets cold, damp. I have a sense I've felt this before, a long time ago. I feel excited and scared, but I don't know if it's a memory or the present. I continue walking.

Where are we? Do you know where we're going? Olwyn sounds scared. Her voice shakes. She's wadded my shirt in her fist. I stop and turn to her. I hold her. I put my face to hers and I kiss her on the head. I turn and continue our descent. The creatures back here are helpful, I say, LaMore is afraid of them.

The floor levels off and I sense them. I put my arms out. The hallway has broadened, the air is less constrained. Maybe we are in a room, but I can sense them. I've been around them enough to know when they are near. Hello, I say to the void. You are with the girl, and you are alive. Where are we? You are with us. Olwyn and I are latched to each other. I am not sure if I'm afraid. Olwyn's fingernails pierce my skin. A dim light rises in the room. Shadowed figures are all around in the large space. I can't see any features, where faces should be is dark, sometimes blue, other times green, grey, black or white. One is blood red. They stand like humans, have shoulders but no arms, legs indistinct as though draped by a robe.

We've been wanting you here, voices speak in my

head. We knew a time would come and you would be here with us. You are their next evolution and we need to see for ourselves. We need to know what they are planning.

Can you ask them or spy on them?

We are not in a hurry. We wait and we watch. We could take them and the humans today, but we wait. We wait for them to pave the way. A human analogy would be waiting for a fruit to ripen. It is sweeter if you wait to pick it.

What the hell are you guys? Olwyn says. What the hell do you want with us or those creepy tentacle guys?

We've been here for hundreds of years. We have learned about you and we've made it possible for the others to settle. Our hand is always invisible, their success is ours. They will do our work for us, we are certain. You are part of us becoming certain. Humans like you are what they want and we need to know exactly why. We need to know what you are made of before we make a decision to let them continue. We could devour them today, but the fruit would be sour and our race would not thrive as we wish to thrive. Once the humans have been transformed we will feast and we will ascend to our next stage of evolution, but we need to be sure.

My arms lock to my sides. Olwyn yells obscenities. My legs lock and the creatures pick us both up. A hand passes over my body and my clothes are sliced open, they fall open. The air is warm. I am exposed but comfortable. Olwyn's body is beautiful. Her hair looks like a ball of fire, her spirit rages against fate. They carry us to another room and lay us on tables. We are surrounded and observed, paralyzed. Olwyn whimpers. I want to comfort her. I want the comfort of her.

You will feel no pain and we will block any images which might cause you undue distress. They have not yet transformed you, but you've both been touched. You still have human weaknesses and are easily harmed. It is not our desire to harm you, we leave that for the others, but we need to study. Olwyn argues, her green eyes blaze. It is true that you will die and we see that is a harm, but you will not suffer. We are certain of that. We see through you. We can read all of your nerves. In fact, you have pain that you are unaware of. We will take that away right now. All of your trouble and worry and whatever has blocked you in the past will melt away. You will be as pure as humans can be. This is not a drug, we are setting you free

I feel a lightness in my spine and through my body. Weight drops away hundreds of pounds at a time. My vision feels clearer.A deep, hearty laugh arises from me that is so hard and robust that my sides hurt. I am more alive than I ever knew possible. Olwyn laughs a crackling laugh, too. She moans like in sex and she laughs. I feel it too.

I feel walls fall down in my mind and body. I remember who I am. I am from Boise, Idaho. I was a musician and I did a lot of drugs. I fell down a flight of stairs in an overdose and I lost my memory. I wandered in a haze for weeks. I hitchhiked and walked down random highways until I reached Portland and LaMore. It is so sad to see my life like this; it unfolds like a story in a book. My mother was a beautiful woman and my father was strong and handsome. They were heartbroken when they found me asleep with a needle in my arm that cold Christmas morning. I'd been a good kid, creative and rebellious. My experiments got the best of me when I got a taste of opium. I couldn't fight it. I was defeated the first time. I feel the pain of the losses and the shame of the betrayals, but I hold them like children and they melt into love. I see my parents' faces floating before me. I can no longer touch them.

I have a name. My name is Jack Solomon. I am whole, a man re-made on his cold, hard deathbed. The creatures move around the room. Olwyn is the woman I love and she is naked and a vision of beauty. Her eyes are open and blinking. She says that she loves me and I say I love her, too. She laughs when I tell her my name. She says I look like a Jack. They release our arms and our hands lock. She is warm and soft. We lie on our tables, she tells me how life is perfect, how ending with love is the best that anyone could ever hope for. We live and we die, we all die, she says. Dying with you is the best possible thing I could ever do with my life. More time would just be more time, we could never love each other more than we do right now in this perfect moment. You are the smartest girl I've ever known, I say, you set me free. Without you, I'd still be with LaMore, dead every day. She clenches my hand. This is it, she says to me, this is goodbye, lover. Her final words are: I see the end.

Her eyes close in slow-motion, her green eyes fade. There is no sound in my ear. She goes and I feel sadness and joy. I had no feeling before she appeared in my bed. The creatures move around the room. Their heads all shine with color, they are taking Olwyn. They block my consciousness from the pain, I see our bodies as pristine. One final delusion, one last memory gone. Then, when I close my eyes, I see a perfect glass of water on a perfect window sill. The glass has a deep blue tint and it glows in late day sunlight. The sun is setting. I fill with blue light. The sun hits the horizon and shoots straight through the glass and into my eyes. I squint until the final sliver falls below the curve of the earth. It all turns black.

2

Makeover

They call me *O*. They call me *Prah*. They call me *Oprah*. I'm the one they want and the only one they trust to ease the pain of this desperate and pointless world. I'm the only thing that some ever believe in. I am bigger than Jesus and that's no bullshit. I commissioned a battery of polls to prove it. I had a statistician aggregate the data to show, beyond the shadow of a doubt, that Constantine's best character, his finest moment of celebrity creation, paled in comparison to a poor, dusty-butt black girl from Mississippi. I have risen like Jesus never rose. I will continue to shine for eternity because I have the real power behind me. Back from the dead? You better goddamn believe it.

"I am everything." I see my mouth move in the mirror. I look like I'm thirty fucking years old. "I am the universe." No matter what I say, they will believe it and I will look good saying it.

I come and go. I keep the adoring throngs on their toes. I retire. I return. I retire again. I never stop working, but if they don't see fresh video, you may as well be a ghost, which is the genius of the whole deal. I die and am reborn constantly in the public mind. A well-placed vid on the 'net keeps them salivating and the collection plates at my shrines overflow. Today I will return and it's such a fucking rush— this is my favorite part— I'm almost as excited as they are. The world will breathe a sigh of relief when they see me take that stage again. I will rise to my highest level when I dine, when my mouth is large enough to swallow them all.

He enters my dressing room in in the form of a man. I can't give him a name, because that would define him in some way, that would imply that I understand what he really is. Pale and quiet. His dark suit and tie gives him an air of austerity and purity. Fear climbs my spine and grips my lungs; the terror excites me. It's erotic. He sits in the chair as though landing on a cloud. He fills my mind with music. It's grace to res- onate them, our saviors. Not everyone does. Some col- lapse with an aneurysm when the brainwaves collide. I hear Mozart, Wagner, Schoenburg. I've been devoured. I will be devoured yet again. I never die. I have made sure of that. I will remain. I have a date with eternity that begins now.

He rises. His clothes melt and reveal a beautiful body. Tentacles grow from his sides, four on the left and four on the right. His generous cavity opens down the center-line to reveal a vertical mouth full of teeth and small arms. His head elongates to reveal a beautiful, horse-like face. He stretches to eight-feet tall. My breath quickens like the first time with a new lover. I drop my red silk robe to the ground and stand naked before him. I walk into his embrace.

His glands emit a delicious drug that makes my body disappear on a river of bliss and my body floats away. Acids eat my flesh. My skin drips. My organs fall out of my skeleton which crumbles to dust.

Blackness. Sweet dark. The endless void of a pure, eternal consciousness. It is still and peaceful and beautiful. Lights appear and dance around me. I imagine a new body, long legs and graceful arms, more beautiful than I've ever been. It orgasms with each movement. My hands and feet explode with ecstasy. Heat from the lights pushes wave after wave of pleasure through me and it bathes my soul and spirit body. I dissolve this body into nothing and build another, and another, and another. I can be whatever I want to be. I'm a leopard. I'm a dinosaur. My consciousness becomes a single point on the tip of a needle, focused yet diffuse, specific but encompassing every atom in existence.

I can feel them coming. They are light years away, moving fast in physics-defying ships. They move in sprurts. Space-time contracts and they leapfrog millions of years. Then they rest and regain energy for the next jump. I will be here when the fleet arrives. I will help them colonize their new home, I will gather the nourishment this world provides. I lead the humans, but I serve my masters. My transformation will be complete by then. We don't yet know what I'll look like, what my body will be capable of. We're purifying my soul and cleaning my mind. Time dissolves.

I come to on the floor of my dressing room. He's seated and quiet. It's always like this. I feel depleted and refreshed as though waking from a crazy dream. I'm in a body. I am clean. My mind is blown. The space in my skull has increased twofold. My consciousness rattles around like a maid in a mansion. I will fill that space with knowledge just as my body morphs and I become the Queen of the World, the Big *O*.

The Friction of Flight

I take a sip of beer and I wait. Soon, raccoons will sneak across the backyard. I fire practice rounds at the back fence. When I hunt, I wear my black sweatshirt with the hood over my head, mostly to keep off the cool night air, but also for stealth. I am an assassin sent by a Ninja death squad. I wish I had night-vision goggles; the porch light always gives my position away. The stink of extra-hopped homebrew belches don't help. My skills will overcome these obstacles.

The vermin waddle their fat asses across the yard; I tell them to scat, my Southern roots rush back through accent and diction. They don't look my way, steadfast in their pursuit of garbage. They climb over the fence I built to safeguard the compost pile and then they feed.

I know they know I'm not a good shot; we've danced this dance for years now. They know my air rifle won't hurt them. They ravage the compost pile with impunity. They communicate in some supersonic raccoon-speak, laughing at me and my child's air rifle. Fuck you, assholes, I say to them; fuck your fur-coat asses. I watch the projectiles sail and arc limply towards the ground; I nail one in the back of the head, an excellent shot. He whips around and unleashes a guttural, hissing snarl; his eyes gleam, devil eyes in porchlight, he bares his teeth like a little demon. He raises my fear. I grip the gun tighter. I could hit him with it if I had to, but the plastic stock would probably break on his hard head while he gnawed my leg to the bone. He rejoins his family, dining on black banana peels, bumpy avocado skins, damp coffee grounds. I crack another beer and flip the bottle top at him. It trails off into the bushes. This is my life on unemployment.

I drink coffee. I tap away at my laptop. Ruth, my roommate, has gone to work. She kept her job as a math teacher. With so few teachers left, she has to teach all summer for half the wage she'd normally work. Craigslist want-ads have fallen off since the economy tanked. No one needs workers, and I don't fit what anyone's looking for. I look at the labor ads; I don't know a hammer from a hole in the ground. Maybe I could suck in my gut and be a nude model for art students. *Driver Wanted*… I know how to drive. I have a car sitting under the big tulip tree; I'm certain it still works.

The coffee pries my sleepy eyes open. I refresh the page; I have hope. An ad appears. They're looking for a courier – no number, just a blind e-mail. A one-time gig driving a package out to the Gorge, more jobs to come. They put a picture of Bugs Bunny in the ad. Weird. I like weird, and I also like the country. It's a perfect fit. I compose an e-mail response. I have a working automobile... a clean driving record... I'm available and a hard worker. Blah, blah, blah.

Paid work, sightseeing, a day which doesn't slide downhill to the ending scene of masturbation and the 11pm anchorwoman. Maybe this'll shake up my brain, maybe I'll come up with some idea of how to dig myself out of this hole. I can stop by Multnomah Falls on the way back. I've never climbed to the top, maybe this is the day for an extra challenge. Damn, I sound like some chipper, hopeful asshole. I send the e-mail and attach a picture of the Road Runner as a retort to their Bugs. Why not?

I post an ad offering art lessons. I apply to work in a retail hellhole. I customize my resume to substitute teach in a private school. Futile, futile, futile. It's not easy being an unemployed art teacher with a chip on his shoulder. I wish I could jettison my sense of right and wrong and do whatever job came my way. Maybe I dropped too much acid in my younger days, or maybe I read too much Nietzsche, but the thing is I can't help but see through false bullshit.

I check my profiles on the online dating services. No responses. I guess it doesn't help when I list my occupation as "not applicable." Futile is sorta the same word as feudal; maybe we can reinstate that system. I can be an artist for some rich banker or oil baron, my contract will signify a free choice. I can choose to lick his ass or die in the streets. Freedom. Fuck it, that'd be great. Bring it on, I say to the cat. She has her back to me, tail raised and crooked like a question mark.

◇

I sit on the sofa. Idle. My heart starts to jump in my chest, the rumble of joblessness; homelessness; insanity; disease; death. This involuntary panic happens once a day. There's nothing I can do about it but try to be comfortable in my immobility. It's an aftershock, a leftover tremor from the day I was fired.

The e-mail chime goes off. The courier people have a phone number for me to call. This plot is thickening. The very idea of money brings a sense of ease. I dig my phone out of the sofa cushions.

"Yeah?" A raspy voice says.

"I'm calling about the courier gig. You need a driver?"

"You got gps?"

"I have a map."

"Your car in good shape?

"She's a peach," I say. "I've got all the insurance and stuff here."

"That's okay, we know all we need to know about you," he says. "You're exactly what we're looking for."

"What do you know?"

He skips my question and gives me an address. Nice address. Sellwood. I used to date a girl who rented a basement apartment over there. I search my room and find the car key. I hope the little thing cranks; I haven't driven it in a few weeks. I sometimes forget it's there.

The car is parked under the large Tulip tree, where those damn raccoons live. I figure that, even though the paint job is oxidized, it's good to keep it shaded. I walk out to the car and something looks odd. The paint isn't the normal dull matte. It's textured with tiny bumps, it's shiny too. The tree has been leaking sap onto the thing for weeks or months. I unlock the door; it needs an extra tug and opens with a suction sound.

I find the man's house hidden behind trees and bushes overgrown with neglect; the weeds are knee-high, but the walkway is clear. A middle-aged man with a large white beard sits on the porch smoking a pipe; a brown ring circles his mouth. A black cat lounges sphinx-like on the wide railing. A baseball game wafts from tinny transistor radio, three balls and two strikes. The man is a Santa gone to seed, a skinny elf in a down economy. His overalls are baggy and loose. The cat trots away.

"Hello," I say. "I'm the guy found your ad."

"With the Roadrunner?" The man laughs. "That thing your car? It damn sure ain't no muscle car."

"It ain't a racer, but it runs."

"It looks funny."

"It's a Honda."

"Looks like it's got lizard skin. Wait here."

I take a seat on the mildewed sofa and the man

slips through the door kinda sneaky-like. There's a four foot stack of newspapers inside the door, it's dark inside. A bedsheet covers the far window. The door shuts. The cat reappears and eyes me. I scratch the armrest and it steps closer. The man comes through the door with an old television box, color, 27″, made in USA. Antique.

"That's Marvin, my cat," he says, balancing the box on the porch rail.

"I'm Griffin, by the way." I extend my hand to shake, but his hands are full.

"Melvin," he says. "This is the package. It's not heavy. You need to take it to The Dalles, out that way."

"No problem."

"Look, here's a card for thirty bucks of gas. Use the station up at Holgate, no other. Thirty should get that car there and back in that thing. There's another card and two hundred in cash when you get back, okay?"

"Yeah, no problem. Where am I going?"

"Here's the directions," he says, scratching his beard, pulling a folded piece of notebook paper from his pocket. He looks me in the eye. "You follow these directions to the letter. No changes. You miss a turn, you turn around and retrace your steps. No shortcuts. Got it?"

"Sure, man, no problem. It's just a package."

"It's not just a package," he says. "This is the most important job you will ever have. Leave your cell phone here with me. That's my security."

"What if I break down?"

"You said your car was in good shape, right?" I nod. "You should have no problems, right?"

"Right." The guy looks like someone's grandfather, I gotta trust him.

"Goddamn right." He pokes his finger to my chest, thumb cocked like the hammer of a gun. "Besides, if you don't show up, someone will find you, don't worry about that." His thumb falls, the hammer hits a bullet, the bullet hits my heart.

The box barely fits in the hatchback, but we manage. It's light, there can't be much in it. He treats it like it was full of fine crystal goblets.

"What is it?"

"That's none of your business," he says. "Your job is to use the directions and deliver it to the people you find there."

I pull out of the driveway. My heart is thumping and my nerves are alight, fear shoots through me. I've never known anything like this. Fuck it. It sure as hell beats sitting around waiting for Ruth to come home and tell me how the school secretary is a bitch. I wish I still smoked. Anything to break the tension.

At the gas station, the attendant gives me a look when I use the card to pay. He eyeballs the card and me. I can't tell if something fishy is going on or if the guy is just a weirdo. It's not like Portland's best and brightest are pumping gas. I might come back and ask the guy for an application.

✧

I pull onto the highway and floor it. My little motor screams until the gears shift and the tension releases, the car launches like a paperclip from a rubber band. A fog of smog poofs from the rear. I go through the next gear and the next, each running to the redline. I feel a tingle from my scalp that goes all the way down my spine. I haven't been out of my neighborhood in a few weeks, or maybe months. It feels good to see Mt. Adams and St. Helens in the distance. I get on I-84 and soon our local volcano, the ever-present threat of molten destruction, Mt. Hood, sprouts on the horizon.

The windows are down, the stereo is screaming rock and roll just like I've played it since I was a teenager driving hell-bent for leather on country black-tops. The box sits in my rear-view, blocking half of the road behind. I can't tell if the blue Ford sedan is one I saw earlier. I figure there's something fishy going on, but its probably nothing.

The world is a suspect now; I'm on a secret mission. This is one of those Raymond Chandler situations where some schnook gets embroiled in a twisted drama, gets the shit kicked out of him a few times, is promised sex and money, but ends up right back where he started – drunk, broke, and alone. I am a pulp stereotype. It's a little after noon and I am not scheduled to show up in any office or other place of employment, I obey no dress code, I have no decent fashion sense. I cross the earth untethered by the strictures of society and civilized people. I wish I were in that movie Mad Max, but with less dust, violence, and more corned-beef sandwiches and indie rock.

I accelerate and the blue Ford stays with me. I slow down and it keeps a distance. I turn up the music and try to block the car from my brain. I try to remember what I learned in that Yoga class Ruth dragged me to, but I can't. It was something about not thinking, but my brain won't shut up long enough for me to tell it to chill out. I punch it up to eighty. The Ford stays with me.

I make good time to The Dalles. I take the exit on the directions. I really want to stop and take a pee at a store, but the Ford has pulled off with me. I don't want to see who's in that car. We fly down the exit ramp. The directions say to turn left. The light is green; I wonder if I'll make it. The blue Ford is either with the old man or against him. Either way, I don't like people on my tail. I let off the brake and accelerate. The light goes to yellow, I put my foot on the brake enough to turn on the brake lights, but not enough to slow. The Ford backs away. The light is still yellow. I release the brake, hit the gas, and squeal through the intersection, the car tilts so much I fear I'll capsize it in a ditch. The light turns red. I leave the Ford at the intersection.

The directions take me up a windy road alongside a small river rushing with Spring snow-melt, a mini-canyon carved in black soil. It's all farm country here at the edge of the desert. Pesticide-rich Christmas tree farms, berry farms, and free-range beef for carnivorous hippies in Portland. It's beautiful country, God's country – if I believed in superstitious nonsense. The air cools as I increase altitude.

I can't tell if I've gone too far, if I've overshot the directions. The blue Ford reappears in my rear-view. Maybe it lives here somewhere, they're following me on their own way home. Someone's gotta live out here in the sticks. Every other auto is a pick-up or a 4×4.

The directions were specific, including mileage between turns, but I didn't bother to note the odometer. I read the directions as I drive. There should be a black and white hand-painted sign for huckleberries on my right. I can't remember seeing one. The road cuts back, the curves becoming more dire as I ascend the mountain. I have to slow to make sure I'm on the right road. The Ford stalks. The road dog-legs and I climb higher up the mountain.

Huckleberries. *Sweet Huckleberries* advertised on a rotting sign, matching the directions. About time. I turn down the dirt road and I'm zooming through a forest, the road edges close to marshy creek beds, past a huckleberry stand choked with ivy, and down winding dirt paths. Monstrous trees loom on either side of the road. It's a prehistoric jungle, like the freaking Ewoks live here. I always forget about this shit when I'm in the city living as a quasi-urbanite, hipster wannabe. I used to have students hand in art inspired by all of these hills and trees. That was close enough for me.

The road is a narrow-cut alley between prehistoric trees all bright green in moss, intimidating to my car, their roots bump me around. I find one house, a clapboard shack that looks more like a meth lab than a dwelling. A naked baby wanders alone in the dirt. The second house matches the directions.

A large Victorian, paint peeling and porch wrapped around. The paint looks crappy but the boards don't appear rotted, all of the trim is intact the windows look new and the railings seem solid. The land is cleared of underbrush, the forest floor landscaped and manicured, it looks like a park. There's a rattletrap pick-up in the front yard with no hubcaps and paint worse than my car, but it has a shiny new muffler. A tire swing blows in the breeze. It's a mountain dwelling created by a set designer, ready for Epcot. I notice a goat and a chicken coop to the side of the house. Livestock is a nice touch to complete the picture.

"You got the package?" A hipster-looking guy in a porkpie hat approaches my car. He looks more like a guy from a Portland coffeeshop than a mountain man, but what the hell. I had been afraid I'd find a nest of armed, toothless hicks.

"You the right people?"

"Melvin sent ya, right? Open the hatchback."

"Marvin."

"Marvin's the cat," he says, motioning to the hatchback. "I like that, nice looking out, buddy."

In the rear-view, I see two women striding my way in black ivy hats, big, bubbly sunglasses, cut-off blue jean shorts, and thighs that go on forever. Further back, I see the Blue Ford. I might not have tried to lose them if I knew they were two foxy babes. They look like villains from a retro television show; one has black hair, the other is a flaming redhead. I am a little afraid of them.

"He followed the directions."

"Get the box."

The women lift the box from the back of the car. They rest it on the ground, in a glacial motion as though it held fine crystal goblets.

"You guys have anything for me to take back?"

"What's wrong with your car?" The redhead presses an index finger on the door panel.

"Sap. Tulip tree."

"Looks really cool." The brunette shoots me a shy smile.

"Look. Why don't you come in for a minute? Have a coffee or something," Mr. Porkpie Hat says.

"Sure, I could use a toilet, too."

The house is not the slacker hellhole I expected. The furniture is shabby, but chic like it was picked up from the curb in a good neighborhood. The place is clean, spartan. The floors are shiny-new bamboo and the real-wood paneling was crafted from doug-fir remnants, an artful melange. A flat panel television sits black; smooth, electronic music streams through hidden speakers. The space is scented with jasmine plants. I feel like I'm in a new-age lawyer's office.

"You guys do alright out here, huh?"

"We need to be out of the city, but we love our comforts. We fixed this place up ourselves."

"What do you guys do out here?"

I guess that was the turd in the punchbowl. Porkpie walks off to the kitchen, the redhead turns her back and sat down to read a book. The raven-haired woman takes pity on my faux pas and shows me the bathroom. She waves her head around so I can't see her eyes too well, but I catch a glint under her mane and a half-smile that grabs me in the gut.

"So, I'm Griffin." My heart leaps into my throat. "Say, is there a bathroom I could use?"

"I know." She pushes her hair aside so I can see her full alabaster face. She has a touch of pink in her cheeks and her lips are full. She leads me down the hall.

"You from Portland?" She smells like incense and old wood.

"Nah. I'm from the Bay Area."

"What's your name?"

"Arun, short for Arundhati, the Hindu goddess of night."

"I, uh…" It's too much, I don't know what to say.

"Well, while you think about it, this is the bathroom." She pushes the door open.

I want to tangle my fingers in her bushy black hair, caress her hips; she is beautiful, her strong nose attracts me and her secret smile has a gravity I could be sucked into forever. I want to talk to her forever, I could listen to her soft tones as long as I live. Maybe we can be friends on facebook. She's nowhere around when I come out of the bathroom. Porkpie is sitting on the sofa checking his cellphone.

"Hey, don't say anything about what you did today. You got that?"

"Uh, sure, man," I say. "I'm just a messenger looking for some extra cash."

"Loose lips, man."

"Hey, are you seeing the brunette?"

"You like her?"

"Yeah."

"You'll be back," Porkpie says.

"You think?"

"Hey, wait," Porkpie says, "I got another package. Could you do that? I'll give ya a couple bucks."

"Sure man," I say. "I'm easy."

Porkpie runs and disappears down a stairwell. I wish Arun would reappear, show me to her room. A firm mattress on the floor, a single chair, eerie and unfamiliar music, a stream of incense in late-day sun. I try to imagine what her body would look like in dim light, pale skin writhing and electric.

Porkpie bounces out of the stairwell. He's got a small, oblong package, a soft paper football coated in packing tape.

"Here ya go, give this to Melvin," he says, slipping a bill into my hands. I palm it and stuff it in my jeans.

I'm back to the highway in no time. I'm headed home, back through territory I've covered. I turn up the tunes and pat the package in the passenger seat. Thoughts of Arun trail in road dust.

I've got cash and I met a hot girl and maybe more of this sort of work to come. It's a great day. A weight lifts from my shoulders and fresh air gives my lungs a lightness, my whole body tingles. I turn up my music and whoop at some llamas chewing their cud.

◇

My little engine screams through the gears, launching me into traffic from a short on-ramp. I catch a chill and raise the windows a little. Driving west through the gorge is just as good as driving east, maybe better. Damn, it's a beautiful day. Maybe, in another life, I'd love nature enough to bring a canvas out here and paint alongside the Columbia for the rest of my life. People buy that nature shit.

Porkpie's package rocks back and forth in the passenger floorboard. It was soft like clothes wadded and wrapped hastily. Maybe it's a fake bundle. Maybe there's something precious in the middle, protected by ragged t-shirts and stained underwear. Either way, his money will still buy me shiny baubles, food, or shelter.

A large, black sedan rides up on my tail. Its grill looks like teeth and it bobs up and down like its sniffing my ass, preparing to eat my tiny Japanese auto. I slow to let him pass. He stays with me. I speed up. He stays with me. It's the same shit the girls did to me. I don't know where they hid this car, but then nothing has been exactly normal today. Maybe they wanna play. I'm hoping they'll be with me all the way to Portland.

I floor it and push the little car over 90mph. My

nerves are hot wires thrilled in the speed. The black car stays with me. The car feels unstable, like it could blow off the road. I wonder about the tires. Is the oil fresh? Will I blow the engine? Those girls don't know when to quit. They close in on my bumper even as I push the speedometer to new highs. I've never gone over 100 in any car. My teeth clamp and grind.

Images of Arun push out the panic. My teeth ache for a new reason; her long black hair and creamy thighs topped with cutoff jeans. I wonder how I should play this. Should I try to outrun someone I have no chance of beating, or should I pull over? A million scenarios pass through my head, many involving pushed-up miniskirts and the hood of the car. I figure my motor will blow up if I keep it running it at these speeds. There is an exit coming up, a parking lot with a view of the river.

The girls pull in behind me. My heart races faster and my eyeballs feel like they might blow out of my head. I park with the nose of the car facing a guardrail. The sports car pulls behind me, blocking me in. Sexy, dominant, I think. I bet this girl likes to play rough.

I roll the window down and cut the engine. I knock the seat back a notch and feel the river breeze. The car sits still. Its windows are tinted, a solid black entity blocking my path. Its engine idles. I start looking around to see how I can get out. This game is going on a bit longer than I'd like. Last time they got right out of the car, didn't they?

I hear the driver side door open and I see a man with waxy-white skin emerge. He's wearing a black suit.

His hair is shiny and black, it looks like a solid mass, a skull cap. He looks at me, catching my eyes in the mirror. I hear a buzzing deep in my brain.   This shit ain't right.

I get out, nervous. I stumble over my own feet. I make it out. The man is coming towards me, but his body is still. He floats, glides over the pavement.

"What the fuck do you want, man?"

He comes for me and I run around the car. He's fast. Fuck. I don't think I'll be able to get away, the car is blocked in; this is checkmate. Fuck it, I gotta get away so I leap over the guardrail and scramble down the hill, through weeds, gravel, and scrub brush. I lean back into the hill, sliding, and make it to the rocks below. The buzzing becomes a screeching feedback loop piercing through my brain. The man is still up in the parking lot, black eyes watch me; he stands motionless.

I run, stumbling, along the shore. I fall in the river. The buzzing subsides after a few hundred yards. I guess he wasn't so interested in me after all. I hope that package wasn't too important.

I stick to the river and have to guess which little tributary the house was on. I figure I'd been on the highway for three miles or so, so after an hour of stumbling along the shore, I turn right and climb through a dark tunnel to follow the large creek. Branches tear at my face, hands, and clothes. I'm soaked from falling in the water. That goddamn old man took my cell phone, asshole, but it would've been ruined in the water, anyway. Why do I need to go back? These jerks got me in this trouble in the first place. They're gonna be pissed that worm-man stole their package, but I'm fucking duty bound to go tell them what happened. I just hope Porkpie doesn't want his money back and Arun won't think I'm a fool to fall in the river. Maybe she'll want to give me a blanket and make me hot tea.

When I can see above the rim of the gulley I'm in, I think I'm seeing the other side of the fields I passed earlier, but I can't be sure. All of this nature has me confused. The trees look the same, the berry fields are identical. I can't believe I answered a goddamn Craigslist ad that landed me in a fucked-up situation with freaky people. I'm miserable and wet and it's as likely a bear will eat me as I am to find my way back to Arun. The odds flip-flop where the chances of getting with her are concerned. I've probably lost my car forever, my life is in danger, and I still don't have a goddamned job.

I come around a tight bend in the river, tromping and cursing in the water. The sun is getting low in the sky, and in a orange shaft of light I see a Blue Heron. Everything goes still. It's about fifty feet from me, standing still and majestic. I hear myself breathing, a twig snaps in the distance. I don't care much about birds. I don't know a Parakeet from a Penguin, but a Blue Heron is self-evident. Large, statuesque, blue. I was dating a hippie outdoorswoman when I first saw one; we were exploring protected wetlands, reveling in silent righteousness, and the thing launched from reeds mere feet from where we stood; it sprayed me with marshwater and, in that moment, the whole world became real and I saw myself as a part of nature, that it could affect me. It's still sorta magical to see one of those big, blue birds. I'm stopped and floored, awed by the forest and the power it holds.

The bird flies away, its large wings beat the air and I hear the wind resist. This is the friction of flight: clawing through air, grappling all the way to heaven. With the bird gone, I refocus to see the house in the distance. I'm sure it's their house. Thank god I can get out of this creek.

"Hey, what the fuck happened," Porkpie's voice from behind a screened door. The door bursts open and he's on me in no time.

"Some fucked-up-looking guy came after me."

"Figured as much. We have to haul ass."

He grabs my arm and turns me towards a car. I feel like I'm five years old and late for church.

"Hey, what the fuck?"

"The fuck nothing," Porkpie stops, drops my arm. "I've been waiting on your slow ass. They took the bait."

"Bait?" This motherfucker set me up.

"Be happy you got away. Get in the car."

"Well… I." I just wanted to make a little money. I'm ready to go home.

"Get in the car."

✧

Porkpie's car is a serious machine. An old-school sedan with a supercharged motor. He plays industrial heavy-metal so loud I think my ears are gonna bleed. He navigates the corridor of trees without a waver.

"What the fuck, man?"

"Those guys, that guy you saw," he says, cutting the tunes.

"Yeah?" I say, "There are more of those freaky motherfuckers?"

"Yup," he says. "No one knows about it. Now you know."

Cool as a cucumber, he speeds through a steep curve, it feels like we're on train tracks. Halfway through the banked ess, I'm pressed against the door, he leans over to the glove box and pulls out a heavy-duty pistol. He holds it vertical, bisecting his face. His eyes drill into mine, unblinking. I can't tell if he's gonna shoot me or him and I don't know which I care more about.

"You gonna fucking shoot that thing?"

Porkpie laughs, his body melts into an easy posture and tosses the weapon at me. I bobble the heavy, cold black steel. It rests in my hands and I know what the feeling of power is. I have never held a gun with bullets, not real bullets. Stage guns are similar, but this one could blow a hole clear through Porkpie's skull. For real, no games. I like this feeling, holding life and death. I pull back the hammer. Oh fuck. I cocked a goddamn cannon. I can't speak. I look over at Porkpie.

"It's not loaded," he says. "I cleaned it myself this morning. Ammo's in the glove box. I just wanted to fuck with ya. Here, this is more your speed."

Porkpie hands me a cellphone-looking thing which is tracking a red dot on a map. He accelerates through a tight mountain curve.

"Where are they?"

"Looks like it's out past town, somewhere in the mountains before the ocean."

"Kinda figured," he said. "We've been able to narrow them to a general area, but now we'll know for sure where they are. Thanks to you."

"Well, what if I had outrun him?"

"Don't be silly."

"What was in that box I brought you?"

"Styrofoam peanuts and a porno mag. Inside joke."

"Hilarious."

"Mind if I call you 'Punch Line'?"

"Fuck you, man." I point the gun at him. "I'll call you 'Porkpie.'" I pull the trigger. The hammer falls on an empty chamber, *click*.

We hit the highway and Porkpie slams the gas pedal and the center line becomes solid.

"Hey, there's where I left my car." The world is a blur and I can't tell if I see it or not. It might be behind a fir tree.

"Time to forget it."

My stomach knots at the thought of losing my car. It's carried me a long way and I'm attached to the oxidized paint, the rip in the driver seat, the funny way it cranks in winter. That thing meant more to me than any human, except for my roommate, that is. I'm a lonely son-of-a-bitch. I'm unemployed, inept in relationships, distrusting of most people, places, and things – except for that small Japanese car which never let me down.

"We'll get you new wheels," Porkpie said. "You survive this, you'll get whatever car you want, maybe even your old car if we find it."

"Looks like our package found a home." The red light is stationary.

"Good. Save those coordinates, we've got shit to do."

We get back to Portland in no time. I'm thinking of going home and leaving Porkpie to his adventures alone. Guy's kind of a dick. Besides, I'm starved, in need of a beer, a bong hit, and a nice session of mindless video games. Tune out. Fuck all this cloak and dagger bullshit. The goddamn world can end, the terrorists can win, Wall Street can become my big-dick daddy, I don't fucking care.

"Strip club?" Porkpie pulls off the highway. "I'm buying."

"Now you're talking." My allegiance is so easily won. "My main man, Porkpie! Holy shit!"

◇

The club has that late-day look, it'd be happy hour if this weren't a place for the lonely and desperate. The neons glow dim, sunlight streams through the windows. If I were a better painter, I could figure out how to capture this light on a canvas. Porkpie orders two ales from the cocktail waitress. A single dancer sways naked on the stage, her pendulous breasts swing behind her body's movement, her eyes stare a thousand miles over us and the only other guy in the club, some black guy who scribbles with an intensity you'd think would burn the paper. I remember now why I never come in here.

"See that woman there?"

"Yeah?"

"She was a dancer here the other day," Porkpie says. "Today she's the owner."

"American Dream, huh?" The beer is pretty good, it's hoppy and the scent opens my nasal passages.

"The former owner disappeared."

"So what?"

"So, she's in on it, she's one of them."

"Like that guy in the car?"

"Naw, human." Porkpie takes a deep draught of the beer. "Human for now, that is."

"Like some bodysnatcher action?"

"Something like that."

My jaw drops. Arun. Like, half-naked Arun strutting silent and confident to our table. She's in a bikini and stiletto heels. I kind of expected a few candlelight dinners with my special spaghetti sauce before I'd be able to see this. Her legs are strong; I like how she bites her lip.

"Yeah, she's taken over."

"See any of 'em?"

"They're all around, I think they're trying to get into my mind."

"Here's $20, go in the room with her."

"Me?"

"She's like my sister," Porkpie says. "You look like you need titties."

The private room is nothing but a closet with a comfortable chair, sloppy red-painted walls, and dim light. Arun sways and unhooks her bra. Her breasts open to the air, fall a bit, and stare at me. It's too much, I'm about to jump out of my skin. She's kind of clumsy, but she has a charm I can't deny, her fumbling sexuality endears her to me.

"Look, here's what I found," Arun drops her panties on my face, something hard hits my nose. She whispers low-sexy in my ear. "Be sly, sniff, 'em, but get the drive out when you put them in your lap. There's cameras."

Her panties have the soft feminine silkiness I've been missing. I rub them on my face to make a good show, but it's luxury, it reminds me of what sex was like, what women are like. There's a secret pocket, I palm the drive, and I slide it in my pants. How I wish this weren't a game. She is so sexy.

"Do you like what you see?"

"Yeah." My mouth is cotton-dry and I nearly choke.

I keep thinking she's going to fall over. She is beautiful and my chest is pounding. I'm mesmerized, stupefied in her presence. She looks like she's lost in thought, that turns me on. She could be thinking of her grocery list or French poetry, it wouldn't matter to me. She's a perfect Mona Lisa, holding so much mystery for me. I have a fucking crush. I haven't had a crush in years.

"Ok, that's all," she says. "Did you enjoy that?"

"Can we have dinner?"

"Get my number from Oz," she says. "Keep it on the down-low around here."

"Thanks." I should learn to not say that sometimes.

"What's on this thing?" Porkpie hauls ass from stop sign to stop sign. This is a residential area, for crying out loud.

"Probably nothing new, but we figure any intelligence is good intelligence. Arun is thorough and sneaky. She managed to access their server when she was working a web-stream show. Fools didn't secure their network. Probably didn't think the dancers knew their asses from a hole in the ground. Higher intelligence, my ass."

"Arun's smart."

"Alien fucks, man."

"They're alien?" I know this is dumb the second it comes out of my mouth, but I just don't believe there could be aliens doing this shit. I mean, don't they prefer spectacular takeover scenarios with laser cannons, spaceship attacks, and scary slogans? I can still see that guy staring at me down at the river, I can still feel that scream in my brain. Maybe they'd be reasonable and friendly if we only spoke to them.

"The fuck you think?" He turns in his seat to face me, driving with peripheral vision. "You saw what came for you."

"Plan 9, huh?"

"And worse."

"Man, how are we so sure about that?" A child rolls into the street, unaware of danger, pedaling a red tricycle. I clench from my toes to the top of my head. Kid can't be much more than three. Porkpie stops with plenty of space. the child looks at the car with saucer eyes. Porkpie taps the horn. The child starts bawling and then the neglectful parent materializes to snatch the kid and shoots us a look of rage. "I mean, aren't there supposed to be good aliens, like ET or My Favorite Martian? Fuck, you know what I mean."

"There doing a sort of hybridization with humans, we're trying to figure it all out. All we know is that this is bad for humanity and it's gotta stop."

"Right on." I'm not sure if changing things up a bit is such a bad idea.

It's a long way from out of work art teacher to savior of the planet and my stomach feels like a balloon animal – full of air and twisted to violent contortion. Pressure is building inside of me, I feel light headed. This shit sucks. Why can't I just go home, smoke a joint and wait for the world to end? Knowledge is so heavy sometimes. I can deny my tactics for avoiding relationships, my drinking problem, or any number of things. They are the stuff of analysis, conjecture, and opinion. But, when it comes to a problem like this, I can't bury my head in the sand, avoid the facts, and suppress my own instincts. I just can't.

I want this to be a hoax. If something were going on as bad as Porkpie says, there'd be real shit happening. Bread lines. Roving bands of cannibalistic rednecks, bombs going off at random intervals, curfews, and a military state seeking to suppress the invasion. But, there's not much other than a lot of unemployment, finger-pointing, no solutions, and little hope for the future. Humans are being turned into mutants and we've got the status quo. Maybe this is exactly what the end of the world looks like. A fucking whimper in a dark and lonely night where no god or goddess is going to save your ass. It makes sense. No one really gives much of a shit except for whether or not they get a new car, if their show is on television, or of they can get laid by the hottest piece of ass in the room. Meanwhile, things go to hell. Those that could do something act if it benefits their short-term agenda. The media cover the bullshit they're told to cover, they create conflict and controversy for an apathetic populace who only seek temporary relief from the illusory strains of life. I need a handful of sedatives.

"Where we going?"

"The old man's place." The car flies like a bullet train. "I want to wait for nightfall."

Melvin's basement is a mess of wooden work tables, rusty tools, screws, nails, washers, wires, and one corner full of high-tech computer equipment, a HAM radio, mute tv monitors, and a few threadbare office chairs from the 1970's whose rollers sink into a jagged square of leftover shag carpet which reminds me of my last trip to a sleazy motel. Wires run down the walls like a cascade of snakes.

Seedy Santa doesn't move when we enter, he sits at a computer, hunched over and watching a black screen full of green numbers which float up and down the monitor, carrying abstract meanings. I am reminded of hieroglyphs.

"Here's your phone, kid." Melvin pulls my phone from a desk drawer.

There are messages. I go weeks with nothing and then today, of all days, when it looks like the end is surely near, the whole world reaches out to me. Schools have called me to interview, a few parents want me to tutor their kids, and there's a portfolio request for a free-lance gig. Weird. I asked for a job and today I got a job. I may have more jobs than I ever intended or wanted. The world is so strange. Just when things seemed the most dire, there is salvation. But also looming destruc-tion. Fuck. This isn't even a guess or a paranoid fantasy. We are doomed and for some reason I was fated to be wrapped up in the middle of it. Knowledge sucks.

"Shit. Hey man, got Arun's number? She said you'd give it to me." Hell, if I play my cards right, I might even have a girl to watch the carnage with.

"Sure." Porkpie hands me a card with her name and number on it. "Hope you get a chance to use it."

"What do you mean?"

Melvin swivels in his chair. He stares up at Porkpie with his hands clasped on his belly. "This is the night, kid. We can't wait. They'll know we've located them and I ain't waiting around to see if they can track every-thing back."

"What's the plan?"

"Got another errand for ya, kid." The old man's eyes are hard and focused now, his posture is stiffening.

"What if I say no?"

"Say bye-bye to Arun," Porkpie looks me square in the eye. "She don't like pussies."

"There's other girls."

"The fuck you talking about? Here's the address, ask for a guy named Bino and he'll take care of ya.

It's just a box, nothing weird. This one will be heavy, though. Real heavy." Porkpie nods in agreement with the old man and they give each other a look.

"Here, kid, it's around back. A little green car, kinda like yours." The old man pulls a car key from the breast pouch of his overalls. It's on a bugs bunny key ring.

I gotta schlep to St. Johns, a far-north part of Portland stuck out on the Peninsula, isolated from everything, and across a majestic green suspension bridge which connects the quasi-suburb to a verdant shore. The gothic supports tower over me and I can hear church bells in my mind, imagined portents of doom. The downtown area reminds me of a little hick town from back home. Longshoremen and junkies roam around here, both inebriated on their poison of choice. The shipworkers supply black tar from Asia and spend their money in the bars. It's a great little economy. When I dated a woman up here, her dogs found balls of junk. They ate the drugs and died.

I find my destination. It's a small house next to a large wooded park. The door is red and the grass is overgrown. It looks like a drug house. I half expect to find a room full of nodding addicts, but a nervous guy opens the door. He's short but made of pure muscle and tattoo ink. He has his hand on the hilt of a huge knife he wears on his belt.

"What?"

"You Bino?"

"Who sent ya?"

"Is this some noir movie? Melvin sent me."

"Dunno Melvin, I know a Marvin."

"Marvin is the cat."

"I got what you need." He opens the door and walks into a darkened room. "Take a seat."

I sit in an deep green easy chair closest to the door. The furniture is arranged in a dark rectangle and a glass coffee table sits in the center, reflecting a shard of light from parted windowshades. A waifish girl leans forward, diving into a shaft of light, her head moving with pure intention towards the coffee table. Her ribcage shows from under a skin-tight tank top. Her face is obscured by stringy, matted hair which hangs. She snorts. Must be doing speed, I reckon.

She pulls her body upright in a whoosh of inhale and greasy hair. She exhales out of her mouth in a throaty hiss, her body slinking back to the shadow.

"You want a line?" Bino's voice is at the end of the hall.

"I don't know, man."

"You're not a fucking cop are you?" His voice is an octave lower, the consonants clip like a drill sergeant.

"Ah, yeah, maybe a bump, I'm not one for speed, man," I say. "I'm more of a doobie guy, you know?"

"She'll get you a bump," Bino's voice relaxes. "You hear me, Trixie?"

The girl doesn't say anything, but she reaches into the light for an amber vial, opens it, and dumps a bit of powder on the glass. She uses a razor to chop the drug into a finer dust.

"You hear me, Trixie?" His voice is deepening again.

"Yeah man, she's taking care of me." My jaw is clamped. I gotta play these people just right. One false move and a character like Bino might explode and then I'd have to scrape a girl's brain from my forehead. "No worries, okay?"

She gestures an offer of drugs. Her face is shrouded in hair, her hands bear tiny scars and the fingernails are nubs. I nod back, not knowing if my shadowed movements register with her, and move forward through air like molasses. She puts a straw in my hand. I don't want to do this. I don't need to get high right now. This is the wrong time, the wrong day, the wrong life for a line of speed. There is more to do and Bino is taking his time.

I look at the straw. Cut to three inches and clean of residue and moral decay. Deep breath. Hold. Straw to nose and dive to the powder trail. Snort. Pow. Zoom. A lightning bolt hit my nose and I'm knocked back to the chair, the back of my throat burns a chemical trail to the center of my life, where all of my fears, hopes, dreams sit, stuck together, in a large confused mass. I see it spinning in a void, making no sense, offering no answer or solace. It glows like a black light in darkness and I can feel the luminescence of my teeth when I smile. I glow, reflecting invisibility as I float in this confused world. Lights shine in the distance, then are extinguished. Faces float up to me bearing teeth, eyes beaming into mine, menacing smiles shock my chest with fear. It's a funhouse, a horror movie unlocked by the white powder voltage on that table.

Sound comes from all around, warm deep tones tingle my skin. The world is a swirl of reds, blues, greens mixed into a muddled mess. This is some good shit. The girl's face appears before mine, warping with words incomprehensible, inhumanely deep then insanely high tones are giving me a message, words, but no meaning. She keeps talking and the more I focus, the clearer she becomes, her words find meaning.

"You okay, man?" She's a dream-girl. Her voice floats on a California ether, her eyes swim, and her smile floats on Cheshire air. I am lost in her eyes. I feel my mouth water, my loins quiver. I could take her this very second, press her to the sofa and give her all my body has to offer. I see those urges, I feel them and know they are real, yet she's not Arun, this is not my night goddess. I wish I could help this one, bring her out of this, give her a shower, but there is nothing in my carnality, no bone to structure the desire of flesh.

"Yeah, yeah." My spine tingles, sensation returns to my body. The room is still monochrome, the air sits, her hair is greasy and matted. I can focus on each of her pores. My nerves are pointy, I crackle. "What, what happened?"

"You were twitching and sorta yelling for a minute. You didn't say anything, though."

"Oh, ok, I guess it's over then."

"We all have something like that happen the first time." She's whispering into my ear, telling me a secret. "One guy didn't know what he was doing and he ran around with his eyes closed until he hit the sliding-glass door. Fucking shattered it. He cut an artery and he died right there. He was screaming for his mother to not die. We put him on Bino's boat and buried him in the river."

"That's very disturbing." The drug is hitting its speedy phase, none of this shit makes sense. "Wait, I blacked out?"

"Bino said he'd be right back, he had to go down the street for something."

"Down the street? Where?"

"He said I should give you a blowjob if you wanted."

"No, thanks." The drugs make it impossible to know if I hide my disgust, or only manage an abrupt politeness.

Her legs extend over the table, feet open with toes spreading and lengthening; her ligaments creak and pop, joints adjust and align. Her toenails are growing, the microscopic hairs bend when the air conditioner roars down on us in a gale. I can't move. If I move shit will happen. She will be able to hear my thoughts. She releases a sigh which lasts an hour, her fetid breath blows hair out in front. Parasites fly from the matted strands. They float away through the ebbing shaft of light. It's a perfect picture of decay in the afternoon, the girl might be beautiful, but I see flesh desiccating in front of my eyes, a spirit wasting to nothing on a sofa with drugs and too much time with nothing to do.

Light blasts in a whoosh of air and Bino's shadow hits the far wall. The girl doesn't move. I don't move. Dust stirs in the light.

"I got what you need." The door slams and dark returns.

"What?"

Bino sits across from the girl on the other sofa. He has a large black case on his lap. He unlatches the lid and opens the mouth of it. and produces an automatic weapon.

"This is the one you wanted, right?"

"Yeah, that looks like it." I have no fucking idea what I'm talking about.

"Good. I already put the others in your car." He pulls out a cigar and puts it in his teeth. "Grenades, too."

The drug can't blunt the impact, my stomach lurches and I feel a knot in my throat. I wish this shit would turn off, that my skin would stop buzzing and that I would stop counting fibers in the carpet. I'm looking at the ground. I'm staring at the spackled ceiling. I am spinning in the space of this living room and I am sitting still. The girl gestures to a white line.

"It'll smooth you out." Her voice is that of a little girl.

Bino closes the case and sets it on my lap. "Get high and get on your way."

I reach for the case. "I'm pretty blasted so I better run."

Bino grabs my wrist, clamps it like a fucking vice. He looks around to the girl, Hey, and she nods to confirm my inebriation.

"Ok, take off," Bino says. "Send my love to that stripper."

◇

I hate driving high and this dope puts a new spin on it. I see cops around every bush, the highway is full of undercover agents and citizens with cellphones, ready to snitch. I get stuck on the 5, at the usual spot, and I have to watch a little boy shoot me time and time again with his toy laser gun. Alien technology, a demon seed, a child ready to turn me in just like his teachers taught him. My skin crawls, but it's more than a feeling. My hands grip the wheel and warp into insect claws; my arms become scaly on the anterior and suction cups form on the soft underside. I know this is false; I know this is false; I know this is nothing but a drug, a trip, a chemical ride into my subconscious, but it won't stop. Breathe, damnit. Breathe.

"That was fast." Melvin scratches his belly and I can hear his organs gurgling under the force of his fingers.

"What do you mean?"

"You were only gone for about an hour." He's grown fangs since I left, he's a vampire Santa. I have to giggle at that.

"That Bino guy is sort of a freak, huh?"

"What's that on your nose?"

"It better be speed," I say.

"Speed? You don't seem jacked."

"It's not like anything I've ever done; I'm seeing shit." The world is full of static noise and eyeballs. A pointillized mouth zooms to eat me, but I know it's a goof, it shatters on my forehead.

"Hm. I bet."

"Got the guns, huh?" Porkpie parts the static and enters the world. He appears taller. He opens a case and pulls out a rifle which glows red in his hands. It's a beautiful, violent red, like blood or demon skin, which Porkpie presently has, smooth and hard like concrete.

"Is he alright?" Voices echo.

"We have a few hours yet, I'm betting he comes down enough by the time you go."

"Huh?" They're talking about me like I'm not here.

"Dude, you're so high it's not even funny." Porkpie's nose is dripping puss. He takes me by the arm and leads me to a bedroom where the late-day sun illuminates an orange blanket draped over a window. "Lie down and I'll check on you when it's time."

The world is caught between two channels, one a fuzzy grey reality and the other a color-negative kaleidoscope, but I can handle it. The nap helped, but I'm phasing in and out of time. All I know now is that I'm in Porkpie's car with a pistol in my hand, there are automatic rifles in the backseat, and it's night. I'm wearing a belt with four hand grenades. Commando. Vigilante.

"You sure you're okay?"

"Yeah man, don't worry." The dashboard melts a little.

Before I know what's happening, we're cruising through darkness, the moon pokes out from behind night-clouds to illuminate a road cut through a fir forest. We crest a hill and below are the bodies of hundreds of trees clear-cut for paper, building, or furniture. Their flattened stumps ooze blood, each sacrificed to the gods of the future, to an economy which doesn't stop growing, its gigantism unchecked and deadly.

"Look at the dead." Words fall out of my mouth. The moon hides behind the clouds and the killing field goes black.

The road twists and climbs over mountains. Porkpie is stolid, intent on the road and maintaining high speed. I have a sense of ease, I anticipate how he will react to each curve. I know I'm in good hands, I know we will be okay as long as we stay on the road. But we aren't going to the shore or to San Francisco or Seattle. We're staying local and we are confronting an evil thing; very few things are worthy of that moniker, a thing has to be pretty big and threatening to merit that degree of badness.

We exit the main road and drive for miles down a dark, dirt-road tunnel. Pedal to the metal, branches beat the car door, startled wildlife sprints out of the road. We pull over by a creek. The air is water-cooled and the trinkling of the water reminds me of childhood camping trips. We don't need words to unpack the weapons. I have enough bullets to take out a small town.

Porkpie motions in moonlight and we head over the creek and into the brambles. The trail is clear and I keep track of him by his white shoes. Fucking second time in twenty-four hours that I've been caught in the woods, without a sidewalk, far from a highway. I don't really care what happens so long as this is the last time I have to pull a briar out of my pants.

We set up at the edge of a field. The silhouettes of cars fill the area, surrounding a large old house, a Victorian mansion straight out of the worst horror movie. The windows glow bright and gold, rays of light cutting the night, palpable. It's inspiring from a distance, I must remember this to paint as a study of light. Porkpie raises a rifle to his shoulder and lines his eye with the scope. I follow his lead.

"Get ready."

The scene is green in the lens of night-vision technology. Greens and blacks and whites render the scene sick, I think of infections and rotting tissue. A car roars into the scene, a large black sedan drives straight to the front stairs of the house and stops on a dime.

"This is it." He chambers a bullet. I chamber a bullet. I hear him take a slow, deep breath. He inhales a bit more, then more still. He must be about to pop. The air begins to seep out of him when his gun erupts in a flash and clatter. Puffs of dust rise around the car. I clench and stiffen. I can't move. I can't breathe, or I can't catch my breath. I'm drowning. His weapon stills. He whacks my head. I shake my head, I feel my lungs again.

"Fucking fire. Or else, man."

I look into the green haze. Men are scrambling all around. They are moving in our direction. My fear of death overwhelms my fear of action and I squeeze the trigger. I think I hit a few. I take single shots, measured snipes on an unknown enemy. My accuracy surprises me and I keep firing, firing, firing. Dark figures stream from the door of the house and I pick them off one by one. I fire a few through the windows, hoping for a random hit. Porkpie throws a grenade under one of the cars, blowing it sky-high in a ball of flame. A second set of weapons appear at the far end of the field.

"Backup has arrived," Porkpie says.

I throw one of my grenades as far as I can. Two cars burst into flame. My shoulder aches from the kick of the gun. I reload my weapon and keep firing. Time is frozen, I see myself from outside my body. I know I'm scared shitless but my mind is empty, my body is machine. The bullets fly from the barrel, my focus is unshaken by explosions, I'm inspired by the other nest of snipers, whoever they are.

The men keep pouring out of the house, like a clown car with some hidden compartment, a hidden bunker of freakazoids. They fall just like everybody else. I train my sights and fire into the brain of one and something tugs my ankle. Then the other ankle. I bend my knees to entrench myself. Something runs up my leg, wraps my waist, I struggle to aim but I am overtaken by a tentacle around my neck. I look over, Porkpie is on the ground being dragged and I fall towards him. My head is covered and the prick of a needle burns my ass.

✧

I have woken and slept and woken and slept. I sit in the dark. Sometimes there is music. I pace around the room and listen to whispers, I talk to ghosts. Food is passed under the door and I eat with my hands. An unseen hose washes me.

The door opens and she is here. We can still speak and the sound surprises us, it shocks us back to our bodies. We make noises when we run out of words, babblings like babies, to hear a human voice in the dark. Meaning has no importance, all we have are moments and it's her energy I crave, her heat warms parts of me that mere words and intentions and kind gestures never could. It's Arun, she says so, I tell her it's me. Her hair feels like what I imagine. Her body is what I want. She has been pregnant with our child and they have taken it. We have had three children. One was born alive, in the dark. When she told me, she wept in my arms.

We have long visits, clinging to each other, the ache never abates. We cleave to each other with an intensity built in each second of longing. It ends the same way. A whisper of gas chills my spine and we hold tight, we say everything we can say, we say goodbye for the last time every time. We cry and sweat in the dark, my heart collapses under the weight. Her fingers claw my back. The gas hisses, the dark serpent puts our time to an end; I smell it and my eyes become heavy. When she vanishes, my arms collapse onto my chest. I awake in the dark. I float through space. I wait for Arun, my goddess of night, my only dawn.

A Cleaner Today, A Brighter Tomorrow

This girl's gotta get ahead in the world. I could do porn, but I never liked the make-up those girls wear. I could be a model. There are plenty of photographers who would love to take my photo. I really want to want to own a club like where I work, but I don't see how that'll ever happen. Dancers rely on cash, we can't get a bank to credit us for a whole club. My roommate comes barging through the front door like an asshole. I wanted peace and quiet.

I put on my headphones so he can't hear me. So he won't talk. If I don't respond, he can't hear me. So I won't hear him and he won't bother me. I have to wear large headphones so he will see that he is not in my head. I keep my back to him. He can't look. He's always looking. I am a pretty girl. My skin is perfect. I blink five times but he is still here.

I'm stuck with him. Houses don't sell when half the nation is unemployed. I can't afford the place without a housemate. He seemed nice when he moved in. He could pay the rent. He didn't mind when I told him what I do for a living. His eyes are green and his shoulders are thick slabs of meat. He didn't make a comment. His body is lean and veins pop from his arms, pulsing with blood. He tells me my outfits are nice. He stays in his room.

When he traveled to fuck some girl, I hoped he wouldn't come back. Every day he was gone, the radio had a story about a tornado near him. It was just a girl and her dog here alone in the house. I sharpened every knife, twice. I hardly used any extra electricity. I hoped he'd be caught up in a tornado. His body torn limb from limb and scattered all over Oz, or whatever dreamland he comes from. He lives in outer space. He forgets to do his dishes. His face is stubbled and manly. He forgets to put his food back when he's done with it. His witch lives in Oz and he masturbates to a fantasy of her.

I walk my dog. My pit bull pulls me. Bull-Pull. Bully keeps me safe because he is ferocious. His name is Mars, not Bull or Bully or any other thing. Mars. I don't know why I got him. He was a cute puppy and I was lonely. Men are unreliable, dogs are forever. I saw that on television once and it's true. Here he comes again. Calling planet Pluto! He always finds a reason to come down the stairs. I don't think he eats when I'm not here. He clomps like an ape. He wears hats indoors. He's not very smart. He wants food and it takes forever for him to cook it. He doesn't do anything, why does he eat so much? Dishes clatter in his fingers. I sit at my computer and wait. I've told him how to cook faster. He never listens. He is a misogynist. I am wearing a hooded sweatshirt today to cover my face. He tries to peek.

My job requires that men look. They pay a lot to see my holes. Dollar bills fill my garter. I keep my pussy shaved and my tits firm. Men are easy. When I rub against them, they come in their pants and give me money. It's an easy job but the girls keep telling me I'm too old. That's nonsense, but my knees get sore if I work too many shifts in a week. I used to work six nights a week when I was in college. My shifts are in the afternoons. Old men and half-blind drunks have dollars for me. I get some weekend shifts, and clubs all over town call me to fill a spot for a skinny, beautiful blonde. My ass is tight, my tits are rock-hard. Who cares if I'm thirty-five?

At work, I'm Dezi or Desiree. The young girls all want my name, they say so. They don't know it's a French name. It sounds cool to them. They can't use it in any of the clubs I've worked at in Portland. That's a lot of places. Those places all respect me and the work I do for them. The girls shake their cute little hips and their tongues flutter, trying to talk me out of my name. I'm a legend in this town. There isn't enough pussy in Portland to make me give up *Desiree*. No one knows my real name and sometimes I forget it myself. I got used to being called Dezi. I am surprised when my mother calls; she says, bonjour Adrienne. My father won't speak to me anymore. He is ashamed.

I need to figure out how to make more money. Even if I am hot, I will need a new source of revenue for the next ten years or so. I should run a club. My knees won't last long. I have a college degree. I'm smart. Most club owners are just lucky perverts. I can design things. I can write and smile. Pantsuits look great on me. I tried an office job. That didn't work. I tried retail stores and regular restaurants. I'm best at dancing.

I haven't had a shift in five days. In the dressing room, I learn I have a new boss, a Ukrainian named Vlad. He bought the place with human-trafficking money. I know this because I saw him once before. I was doing a side job at a sleazy hotel and my client was late. Vlad was below me, in the parking lot. He had five young girls with him. He pushed them into a van. He had video equipment. A gun was in his waistband. It looked like a Saturday night special, the kind of cheap piece of shit you see on punks.

Vlad is fat. He drinks coffee. His teeth are brown. He has a pimple on his bulbous drunkard's nose. He pulls me into his office. His face is pocked and his head is balding in patches. He is a dog with mange. Vlad says, you need to do more pole tricks. He wants me to bend over and show my asshole more. He knows I'm getting older, but I'm reliable and he can't fire me. He wants to wear me out and make me leave. I'll show that fat immigrant. He says my pussy is worn out. I say, I am hot. I hold my tight titties and press them together. He tells me they are like a cow's udder. I slap my hard ass and he says it is like a deflated child's balloon with stretch marks. I tell him I can pull down $300 on a Monday afternoon. I tell you what, I am nice guy; I do you a favor. For now. He tells me to bend over the desk. I say

I'll never get wet for him. Not pussy, he says, ass. You are disease, I wear rubber.

He stands on a phone book to penetrate me. This is what they're for, now that the internet is on cellphones. His penis is large. I didn't expect that. It takes a while for him to get it in, even with a lot of lube. I have a hard time relaxing my muscles. I say, slow the fuck down, fuckface-motherfucker. He says something in his native language. It takes a few minutes. My asshole opens and he's in me. He slams inside and my stomach feels knotted. I'm bent over a gorgeous rosewood desk, a real antique, an art-deco from the 1930's. His dick is so big it makes me wet. I want to kill this cocksucker. I stare into a knot in the grain, the only imperfection. The desk makes me like the large cock. Hard, hot piston-action in my rectum.

One, two, three, four, five.
Oh, god, give it to me.
One, two, three, four, five.
Fuck me harder, you fucking Russian.
One, two, three, four, five.
I feel a rush of juice and I scream.

I despise my vagina for betraying me. All I care about is the clean, strong desk, its fine grain; it's a boxy and sturdy piece of furniture that doesn't budge. I start to dry out. The finish is smooth and glossy. It cools my cheek and my breath condenses. He squirts more lube, it sounds like a wet shit. I like this desk, I say, one day I'll fuck someone worth a damn right here. He says I wish to be fucking girl worth a dog's balls but all I have is you, Desi. I tell him I'm going to own this place one day. If could shit on his dick, I would, but I got nothing. . I focus on the knot in the wood, the size of a pea, it gets larger the closer I move my eye to it. It's the one weakness in these strong lines, this brilliant design. His body shakes and consonants spew in his gutter language. He pulls out and I fart. I'll shit lube for a few days.

I work and make money. Vlad watches. The cocktail waitress keeps his coffee mug full. He sends someone to buy a dance in the private room. He thinks I don't know. I make the guy bust a nut bigger than he's ever done before. I'm a professional. I bend over at the waist to show a big tipper my stuff and see Vlad talking to some strange guys. Pale men in dark suits. I'm fascinated. Vlad seems afraid of them and I want what they have. I want that sort of power to inspire that sort of fear in a fuckface Russian. They seem to walk, but I'm not sure I see their legs move. I hear murmurs of speech, but I'm not sure I see their mouths move. In the dressing room the girls say they don't like those men. These girls are all dumb hicks.

On the drive home, the sky is a hideous pink. Stupid fluffy clouds float around. I have a wad of cash. Maybe I should start a business. I could set up something in the basement and pay girls to dance online, hardcore streaming shows. I'm a smart, independent woman. I am a beautiful woman. I will find the answer, but I want that fucking club.

Mars barks when I open the door. I feed him. His

jaws are powerful enough to pull a train. They could pulverize bone. I let him outside to crap. I hear clomping on the stairs. I feel queasy. The jerk comes in to cook. I give him my prize-winning smile. My teeth are perfect. I say hello. I say my day was good. He says something about his boring life. I turn away. I go to my room and put on my headphones and the hooded sweatshirt. There is sun coming through the window. I put on sunglasses. He cooks garlicky food. The stench permeates the house. I avoid his gaze. I point to the headphones. He smiles like a jackass. He's wearing pants that bulge. I fix a cucumber sandwich, the vegetable heavy in my hand as I slice it. I take it to my room. I sit on my bed. I'll have crumbs in my bed. I hug my knees and hold my breath. I count to see how long I can go before I pass out. He talks to the dog with a throaty, deep voice. He must be a mental defective. I increase my breath-holding by a few seconds. He clomps upstairs. I exhale. T-shirts and tight pants fill my thoughts. The sweet, sweaty funk when he comes in from a bike ride. I'm wet. I rub my pussy. He can't know what I'm doing. I thrust my fingers inside. He can never know. He wants to know about this. He'd love to watch, he strokes it thinking about only me. I close my eyes and see his face.

I come in a rush of juiciness.

I wash my hands five times to forget.

I need to do something. I need to do something now. I clean. The dog shredded the stuffed monkey I bought. I sweep the stuffing. I mop the kitchen and polish the hardwood in the living room. I wipe my computer monitor screen. I find five books to get rid of. I find three shirts and two pair of shorts I can part with. Five and five in a box at the street. Five keeps me alive. Mother will be proud that I'm purging the clutter. I'll do the garage later.

I want the nightclub. I can run it. The fatass Vlad has no business there. I know this town and how things work. He does not know shit. I must have that club. I must or I will die. This idea repeats. It repeats and becomes a hard knot in my chest. It will not go away until I have what I want.

Vlad calls and wakes me up. He wants me to work. He wants to work me to death. Shower. Make-up. The bathroom is covered in grime. G-string and bluejeans. I feel shame for my life. Wash my hands five times. Sweatshirt and sunglasses. I make coffee for my thermos. I must have the club. I feed the dog. My hands are dirty. I wash them until they are clean. Upstairs is silent. Good.

It's a sunny Saturday. Portlanders don't stay inside on nice days, not even to look at my hot snatch. A few nobodies sit at the bar. I dance in open space. With no tips, I don't show my tits. I sway, hypnotizing myself. I have too many things. I should get rid of it all. It means too much. Special books, the panties I wore when my cousin Francois touched me the first time. I had little tits and fuzz on my pussy. Francois smelled funny. He was scared when I grabbed his small, pink dick. I have tests from college. I need to study them. People will steal my ideas if I throw the old notebooks away.

Dezi. Hey, Dezi. I see Vlad down on the floor. A thin man with pale skin and dark eyes is at his side. Empty tables stretch to the far wall. Neon fades in the sun. Vlad says something about being sexier. I stare at the man. Something is in my head, a tone. It's like when I learned to tune a guitar in music class. The new sound matches the one in my head. The two become one. Vlad's friend is staring at me. We lock eyes. I start to salivate. I feel warm. I don't understand. This is not normal. I can't stop it. I don't want to stop it. Vlad is talking. I don't listen. The man wants to know my desire. I say I want the club. He says I can have it. He says I have to kill Vlad. I say okay. He says a key to the club will be in my car after work. I should kill him soon. Soon is best. Tonight, I say.

Vlad yells at me to dance. I totter and way at half-tempo. I look at the man. He has no expression. He whispers something to Vlad, hiding his mouth, a confidence. I hear it, he tells Vlad it's time to get more girls and drugs. I know what's going on more than Vlad. He looks pitiful now. A customer puts a five dollar bill in my garter. Five to stay alive. I show him my asshole. I open my pussy and show him that. My knees are aching, but I give him a show like I haven't done since I started. I finger myself. I make him smell it. I suck the finger. He is my last customer. He takes out another five and I let him put it between my ass cheeks. I pull it out from the front. I give him a coy-kitten routine and lick the bill, a third makes fifteen. He's the last man to pay for my skin.

I drive around. My minivan makes me look motherly. I stop at a pawnshop. I purchase a foot-long, razor-sharp knife with a bone handle. I buy a sharpening stone for appearances. It's for my husband, I tell the clerk. He likes knives, I say, he'll like it sharp. The clerk puts it in a box. My husband will like that, I say. I flash my million-dollar, award-winning smile. He takes my cash, three fives and the smell of sex parts. He gives me a look. I put my sunglasses on so he won't remember my eyes. I kill time.

The club's lights go out. The last drunk leaves. Girls meet their johns or dealers or jealous boyfriends. I open the box. The blade cuts the cardboard. There is a little rain. Puddles litter the alley. The backdoor light comes on with a motion sensor. The key works. The club is lit with neon signs. Vlad is in his office. Sweat pours from my armpits. I open the door. I hide the knife behind my leg.

Where you been, he says. You leave in middle of your shift, you stupid bitch. You think you have job now? How you get in here?

The pale man is there, sitting across from Vlad. His suit looks fresh at three in the morning. I hear him in my head. No words, but his sound sings with my sound. I know what to do. I say, I'll do whatever you want if you give me my job back. I walk around the side of his desk. I sway and he opens his legs for a lap dance. His arms rest on the chair. I know he's got a gun. I lift my leg and rub his crotch with my foot. He gets hard. I see his eyes go soft. I say, you like that? He murmurs and runs his hand up my thigh, leaning in to reach my dry, cold cunt. His jugular is in my face. I can smell it. The buzz in my mind becomes an aria. He finds my panties. He closes his eyes. I swing the knife and slice his neck to the spine. His eyes pop open. Blood geysers from the artery. I swing the blade backhand. Vlad's head falls to his shoulder, still attached by spine and a flap of skin. The song is so beautiful, cellos chime in, dulcet tones resonate in my pelvis and I'm wet. Vlad's blood streams down my face.

The man is behind me. He tells me to stay still; I close my eyes. My nipples stiffen. I feel a writhing muscle hug my thigh. Another wraps my waist like a constricting snake. A voice rings through my mind, my voice. I am one of them; I am theirs; they are mine. I think of tentacles. I feel one in my front hole. Another enters my back hole. They press deep inside of me. They pulse and slide in and out, first one then the other. A hissing rattle fills the room inside my head. My eyes clench shut. The sound sneaks up my spine and into my head. Both tentacles go deep into me at once and throb in an alternating pattern. I see a bright light behind my eyelids. It is warm. I forget the blood and everything. I start to come. It starts with the light in my mind then moves through my body. I am radiant. I am perfect. I tell the light that I love it. It tells me that I am part of it, I will serve it and it will help me. I come until I collapse on my favorite desk. My eyes can't focus. I could drown in this puddle of blood.

The man helps me cocoon Vlad in plastic wrap. We put him in the back of my minivan. I cover him with trash I carry in the back. The man tells me he will clean the office but I must get rid of the body myself. I shower in the dressing room. Hot water cleans my hair, pink rivulets swirl the drain. The club is mine, mine, mine.

My fingernails are covered in dried red. Bits of Vlad flake off everywhere. The hacksaw is in the garage. I have a plastic bin full of clothes. I force myself to empty it into a garbage bag. Vlad lost most of his blood while I was passed out from coming. Less mess. I hack off his head. I spit in his eye and drop the head like a rotted melon. I separate the limbs at the joints and cut meat from bone. The torso is a problem. I don't have a tool for that. I stab it with my knife. I'm not a good butcher. I go into the house and get Mars. The poor dog hasn't been fed since yesterday. He likes the fat and meat. He doesn't care if my butcher job is half-assed. He's starved and his chewing noises fill the room. Mars loves me so much. He loves me more now that he's got so much fresh meat. I push the torso in his face and his powerful jaws rend skin and muscle from bone in a wet tear. I sit in the backseat while he eats. I am exhausted. I lie down. I fall asleep to the rhythm of his jaws.

The jerk is in the garage. He is yelling and flailing his stupid arms. Mars is barking. The jerk is angry. His anger upsets me. He's wearing a stupid yellow bike helmet. He says, what the fuck did you do? What the fuck is this? I've made a bad mess. I'm a bad roommate. I got blood all over his bike. My teeth go on edge. I look at him and flash my million-dollar smile. I've done the world a favor, I explain. He does not smile back. He does not ask how my day was. He turns to exit.

The knife slides between his shoulders as though through soft, warm butter. There's a slight pop when it pierces a lung. I pull the knife from his back. I grab his hair and pull his head back. The knife slices his neck to the bone. I'm stronger than I think. Maybe it's the adrenaline. It feels good. He twitches. Blood pours all over the floor. Another mess.

I kneel. I look at his eyes. They are hazel and perfect. I've never looked into his eyes. I smell under his arms. He smells of soap and his man smell, sweet and musky. My heart goes hollow. I close his eyes. My vision blurs with water. Why did you have to do this, you asshole? Why did you never make a pass at me? You could have had this body, this beauty, a piece of ass beyond any you've ever known. That would have changed everything. I cradle his head. I cry. His hair is soft; his face angelic as in sleep. My heart hardens and feels like a brick of coal. Tears fall from my eyes into his eyes. Mars' face is in mine, he feels my pain, he wants to protect me. He licks my face. He isn't afraid to whimper and press his body into mine. He can't protect me from myself. I wipe my eyes and sop the dead man's blood.

I lick his lips. He tastes metallic. Mars raises his ears; he'll be hungry again soon.

In Leaves

It's circuit boards and microchips and microtransmitters which look like resistors. It's a satellite network and a spiderweb of data. It's an exotic plant from the Amazon which is shipped in under heavy guard in the middle of the night, processed into the finest white powder, the most potent of its kind, the good shit, the bomb, white kool-aid cocksucking body-blow mindfuck speed, tested in real-world "laboratories," and exported to a global marketplace. It's nothing I could have imagined I'd see in real life. Nothing I've seen on tv or in movies could ever have prepared me for what I do, for what I am, for what I am becoming.

I see what it does, I watch it all shipped out in large brand-name semi-trucks or secreted away in false-bottom trunks. The implements of control, the toys of desire and ease and a modern life in Christendom, the New World. these are what we make and distribute for sale to the outer world, the last world, I fear.

I have days, hours left to enjoy this consciousness, before something else takes over. Today, when I was in the circuit board plant delivering a closed crate, I noticed that my left hand had changed. It has a greenish-bluish hue which seems to come up from below, the color shows through to the surface. The skin looks bumpy, ridges are forming down my metacarpal bones. I handed a package of food to the manager there and we spoke without speaking. The language was music and it was beautiful. Harmonies and syncopation, rhythms and tone. I saw myself reflected in a black-marble eye and I didn't recognize what I saw.

Sometimes, at night, the walls breathe and my heart pounds. I wake in a cold sweat, the shadows taunt me, my back turns to clammy ice. I want you to wipe my brow, to hold me. I want you to let me know that everything will be okay. I am in a desperate state. I have lost the confidence you remember. I am a shell. I host a creature I don't understand. I'm writing this letter to you in an effort to remember what you are and what I was. I am trying to make sense of what I see and what I feel. I walk lost, searching for another that will be as much as you, that will bring me back to a state of normalcy, equilibrium, average middle-class boring bullshit. I'm the only man in a crowd. Emptiness is all around. I am nowhere, the world is a void; even you are nothing. I write to create a toehold on reality, to remember the past and to see the present for what it is, no matter the horror and truth of what I have to impart.

This is a letter to myself, you, and humanity. I've written it on a thousand scraps of paper collected in a box, a jigsaw puzzle of memory, meaning, and outlandish lies. My world feels like a dream or a mad hallucination navigated by intuition, my life is a series of guesses. Whether I offer a false warning or a prescient message is for you to decide, my beautiful reader. My truest wish for everyone is that I am a brain in a vat, prodded by mad scientists, that this only a chemical reaction in a blob of grey matter, the apparition of a world only known to me. I've seen so much that I don't believe, horrors beyond imagination. I do not trust my perceptions. I may be the only person to ever read this. I may never even send it, not even if there were a courier or e-mail available; this confession may only be heard by the thing in my chest that flops and tries to leap out. When the thing molts into adulthood, I will cease to exist. Or I may cease to care, a new set of needs and wants taking my humanity. I have no way to know, no possible expectation, I don't think the thing in me even knows.

ThethingsIhavetotellarethethingsoffantasyand-nightmare.Ihavenotgoneinsane,theworldaroundme-has.OrmaybeIam insane,alostsoulmaladjustedtomyenvi-ronment.Imustwrite.The only hope I have to save my humanity is to write truth on these paper leaves.

I want you to remember me as I was before I left, before my face became scarred, before I lost my hair, before my cheeks hollowed and my arms withered to bone. I see myself reflected in glass and I am a skeletal shadow of my memory. Do you remember the time at the state fair when I heaved a sledgehammer and buried the railroad spike faster than any other man? I write as that man, that is who you should imagine is behind this nub of pencil and these fragments. Hale.

Fit. I want a record to help me remember, so that when things change, this reality will survive as best as I can record it.

If there is one thing you need to know it is this: I am something altogether different, less human or maybe more human. There is something growing in me. I don't know what it is. I write everything so that you understand. I will leave a record of myself before I molt into something horrible.

She spoke French. She played with the little vocabulary she had. It was fun and sexy. I learned a few words, too. One night, she called me "Mon amour." I thought she said "more." I said I'll give you more and I groped her bare thigh. She laughed and growled low and sexy. As we rocked into each other, she said, "c'est l'amour." I said, more, more. I thought she said "say more," I didn't understand. She said, "no, it's love, l'amour." I thrust and she gasped. She said, in breathy moan, "tu es 'L'amour', je suis l'amour, nous sommes l'amour" and she exploded with an orgasm unlike any I've ever seen or felt.

Now, I am more. I am La More.

The desert sun beats my back and the glare blinds me. At night, all heat dissipates into a cloudless sky and I freeze. My thin blanket barely covers me. I shiver to sleep. I am glad that I found a place to stay and I have a bed. I stay alone, apart. Others aren't so lucky.

Maybe it's because I'm quiet or so tall, or because I have a special job that they leave me alone. Sometimes people expect me to lead because of my height, but not here. Here, I am left to solitary, a lone giant.

We were told there would be accommodations. They didn't mention we'd have to fend for ourselves, form tribes, coalitions of anemic animal power, packs of scavengers trolling abandoned subdivisions for a shadow of a life we were taught to expect. Those with better jobs have armed guards protecting their neighborhoods, the lesser of us fear larceny and there are frequently fights, crude knives are brandished.

This was a suburban town. The banks foreclosed on the houses, the city budget dried up and there was a mass exodus. With more time, even the fast-food restaurants and the large big chain stores shuttered. Nature took over much of it. Desert vipers infest homes which once were called mansions and tumbleweeds clog alleyways downtown. The governor called it an unavoidable economic disaster and sold it to my employer.

I drive a bicycle taxi. I carry the managers and I deliver packages, messages, and meals for meetings. I am told to never eat or look at their food. I receive my food at the end of the day, bricks of tasteless protein, vitamin pills, processed vegetable juice. It's hardly enough to last me until morning, they give me the same portion as the shipping clerks who sit around all day. I fear my body is eating itself. Every day I am amazed at the fact of my survival. Each day requires great endurance and strength. It helps to keep my mind silent, any energy lost thinking would mean failure. All day I listen to air whistle past my ears and heave in time with my pumping legs.

I write on scraps of paper I steal when no one is looking, duplicate invoices, used envelopes, even paper bags I cut into page-size pieces. I slip the scraps into my pockets when I make a delivery. The larger bags I slip under the cushion behind me and I smuggle them away under my shirt. The secretaries and clerks are workers with education and skills. They are more valuable to the corporation. They are lazy and don't watch me very closely. I don't know if I'm invisible to them or if they trust me. My betrayal could get us all sent away, but it is only trash that I steal.

There are many versions of this letter. I've found so many ways to tell you what it is like, what I have become, what I have seen and experienced. Each time I write, it comes out different. I use scraps of paper I find and I lose the order. If I knew the date I would use it, but the date was one of the first things I forgot. Some nights I've been too cold and so I've used pages to start fires, those stories lost to the atmosphere, burned to carbon before another eye could find them. Yet, I rewrite and find new words and new meanings, each a fragment of reality I hope will reflect the whole story.

I'll get it right, tell the best truth, so that these are the words that hold the key the to my soul, a poem to make you fall in love with me all over again, to make you sick of me, a document to expose facts and truths with such brutal honesty that you recoil, but which you know to be true in your deepest core.

We've factioned from one another. Tribal sects have formed and hold parts of the town. Some, like the office workers, have their areas maintained for them. Armed guards and electrified fences keep them from us. They drive electric cars in a smug comfort I cannot remember. They are not smarter or better, but they are protected.

The others out here vie for luxury and seek to show themselves worthy of a clean yard and a servant. Each tribe is determined to take what it can from the others. All are kept equally weak, however and when there are skirmishes, the melee is a comic flailing of bony arms, limp-arced stones fly. There are no winners and no losers. I count myself superior, but reality tells me that I am no better. I watch from a remove and no one messes with me. I may be the same, but my job puts me in touch with the Office People and the Managers, so it's assumed that I am a spy. This is just as well. I couldn't stand to be around them for long in any case.

I found the pencil on a shelf, golden yellow and

perfect. My skin tingled when I saw it there, unattended. It had the same glow I saw around your head the first time I saw you. I had delivered a special package and two managers received it. They signed my slip and turned their backs, they were distracted and I knew that would never happen again. The gold called to me. I bored my eyes into their backs and moved my arm without looking at it. My fingers fumbled, but I found it. It slipped and rolled towards the edge. I turned my head and saw the sharp end rolling out over the edge and I snatched it away before it clattered on the floor. I pocketed it and when they turned back to me, my heart raced with panic and pride, they asked if I had anything else. I stammered, no. I can't remember feeling like that since I came home from our first date. I thought he smelled my fear; he didn't say anything or have me searched. I could be sent away for stealing, disappeared into the unknown.

I fear what would happen if anyone found me writing. We are taught to live free, we seek salvation through work, and the joy of serving the corporation.

I've never seen anyone with a book, there is no television and the only computers I've seen are used by higher-level workers and managers. I only want to work and send you money. I hope you receive the money I send, but they won't give me a receipt. They say they are helping the environment, saving paper, and tell me to check my e-mail. When I complain, they refer me to someone I cannot reach who is in a building I'm not familiar with and cannot find. They tell me to trust them.

They say calm down sir, everything is okay, what's the problem? We are all sending money home, that is why we came here, because there were no jobs and our babies were hungry and debt was mounting.

They tell me the telephones will work soon and that I can call and hear your voice. They have said that since I arrived. No one else seems to have a memory, and each time we are told the repair crew is coming, hopes rise. I see the hopeful faces and I despair, but their hope makes life easier for a few days; I luxuriate in the rise in spirit. Soon, routines begin to wear again, we become tired. The rote repetition of tasks hurts. I am fortunate to have my job. I have a few tasks which repeat, but each day brings something new.

One day I was chauffeuring a manager. He kept leaning up from his seat. He grabbed my shoulder and asked questions. They never do that. He was asking about things not related to my job. My childhood, my hobbies, my parents and their lives. He asked about you and my hopes for the future. I told him about how we wanted one boy and one girl. He was very interested to hear about my music; you remember how I played instruments. But the strange thing was how I thought I heard the music, my old guitar playing surf music. That old six-string was always a half-step flat.

Classical instruments rang in my mind. I don't know where it came from, but it wasn't from me. They were deep strings, cellos I guess. I'd never heard the music before, but in my mind I imagined accompaniment. I banged on timpanis and imagined long violin runs cutting straight through the melody. I hate classical music. I don't think I knew the word "timpani" until I imagined them banging away in my fantasy. I surrendered to the beauty of it, the frilliness and pomposity rang through my mind and thrilled my heart. I had no choice but submission. I didn't want to like it. Despite my protest, I was ecstatic in the new sensation. My mind fought my body. I knew something bad was happening, I felt things changing. Nothing has been the same since.

This is where I have to tell you something else. This is something I don't want to say to you, or even admit to myself. That night, I was walking to a house in a subdivision where I had found a mattress in a basement, where I'd been able to store belongings and not have them stolen or destroyed. This is where I still live and write. I was walking home and I found someone on the road, a woman. She was beautiful and in distress, a one-two punch to my heart. I cannot resist those things. So I have not been alone like I may have let you believe earlier, there are some truths I must approach slowly, with care and caution so that I can give birth to them in the time they need, or in a way that I understand.

She has blonde hair and dark skin and her name is Dorsey. That day I found her, she was on the side of the road, lying under a small tree. I asked if she was okay and her eyes were glazed, unfocused. She mumbled and slurred her words, her head lolled side-to-side and she could not move her arms. I picked her up and carried her to my basement. It was a long walk, but the sun was going down, the world cooled. It didn't matter, though, I had new energy, I felt like I could carry anything or walk all over the world and never tire.

When I got her home, I gave her water and she slept for an hour or so. She woke and drank more, at least a gallon. When she regained her strength, she said my name. She'd never met me. She was new to town and had been assigned a job. She said she learned it in a dream. Some sort of tentacled monster told her my name and that she needed to find me. Then the beast devoured her and spat her out under the tree where I found her. I said that dreams are weird things, but I thought it was unusual how she knew my name. It's not like everyone is named Teague.

That night, Dorsey slept in my bed. I reached for her; she reached for me. We satisfied each other but we weren't sated. We clung to each other with raw muscles, our hands hungry claws, our teeth gnashed; we were wild animals fighting over a scrap of gristle, but neither could destroy the other. I tore into her and she into me, our chests opened to each other. I was inside her, this is the physical truth. But she was every bit inside of me, I was penetrated and defiled and dominated though those were my hands pinning her to the ground, pulling her hair, making her squeal in the night. Her grasp constricted tighter around me, stronger through me. Even now, when I come within a few feet of her, I smell her blood; the pump of her heart throbs as though in my own body.

She is still in my bed at night. We keep each other warm, and every night we claw at each other, our bodies expending every ounce of energy, trying to slam our souls into each other. It's as though my inner being is pressing against my skin, straining to break through and devour her and she me. This might sound like the sort of thing that lovers say, a poetic description of hot sex, but this is the truth as best as I can report it. There is something growing inside me which is trying to get out to meet something inside of her.

After she appeared, things started to change for me around the town and at work. Wherever I go to deliver packages, people seem happier to see me and the managers give me long, silent stares which I sense indicate an interest in me; they used to ignore me or suffer through our exchanges until I left.

I arrived after a long bus ride across mountains passes, through a hundred small towns, and to the hot, arid desert. We took two lane highways the whole way and it felt like the ride would never stop, each day blurring into the next. The old man next to me slept the whole time, he slumped onto my shoulder and murmured about someone named Lucky, maybe his dog, or maybe he dreamed about gambling.

There are no evergreens here, there is no moss, and it never rains. What I remember most about the bus ride is driving at night, my reflection in the glass, subdivisions or office parks on the horizon.

They woke me at dawn when we arrived. It was already 90°. They divided us into two single-file lines. Men in one, women in the other. We each had our own entrance into a small cinder-block building with no windows. No one said a word and no one made eye contact. There I was with all of my fellow newcomers; no one seemed excited to be there or interested in discussing the heat or how different the cacti were from Douglas Fir. Our Northwestern friendliness was sucked from the room and we were nothing but bodies, cattle in a pen. I see now that that's what we are, all of us. We are stupid beasts with little more than animal instincts, bags of meat with selfish desires wrapped in oil-based garments, fake spirituality, hypocritical belief systems.

In the building, we were questioned. They demanded our basic information. Then they wanted more. Marriage. Appetite. Sex habits. What of books, movies, religion, friends, cars, goals, and dreams? Each one of us provided an inventory of our lives, what photographs we had were scanned and catalogued, our personalities cross-referenced and cataloged in a database somewhere. Cattle. Sheep. We did it to work to feed children, lovers, make car payments, mortgages, then support our parents in their old age. We did it to be the same human as the schmuck next door with the revolving door of bimbos and sports cars.

I tried to stick with my seat-mate from the bus but he was shuffled away when they took all of our basic information. The interrogators wore grey jumpsuits and safety glasses. Each had a pistol on his hip. I signed and initialed so many pages and paragraphs I lost track of what it was I was signing. I was asked if I understood and I said yes, yes, yes. Even if I wanted to understand what I was signing and had taken the time to read it all, the print was so small and all the legal language was so confusing that I doubt I would have been any better off. A man to my right asked what would happen if he didn't sign and two very large, burly men escorted him out, so I kept my mouth shut. My head swam, I put my head down. I kept signing the agreement.

They gave me a basic physical exam. The last time I saw my old friend was going into the exam. I never heard him speak a conscious word and I'll never know his name. Maybe he was sick and they took him to a hospital, or maybe he asked questions like the man in the paperwork room.

They took a sample of my hair and a swab of my cheek for a drug test. I told them I smoked herb, but they didn't seem to care. They stripped and hosed me down with a stream of blue chemicals. The smell burned my nose and my skin was pink and raw afterwards. They measured me and they nodded, I think they liked my height and strength. I told them I had no disease nor parasites. They gave me a blank look and sprayed my face with a water hose whenever I thought of asking a question or making a joke or issuing any utterance whatsoever. The solution burned my eyes and the pressure nearly knocked me down. I wanted to fight, but I had no fight. I had nothing but fear. You know that's not like me. Remember when I caused a scene when they wouldn't let us in to *Titanic*? How about the time I mouthed off to that cop at the basketball game? I didn't care about his club, his pepper spray, or his gun. But then, in that windowless building, the words wouldn't come and the anger dissolved. I was paralyzed.

Maybe it was the food they gave us on the bus. It was horrid, but I didn't expect much. Bus food. I'd eaten it and then I slept and then I had no fight. Is it paranoid to think they drugged the food? I think it is, but I've seen so many things here which make adulterated food seem like small potatoes. I question my own perceptions, but the point is moot. What I am, what I know as me, is going away more every day.

Maybe I didn't throw a fit because of you. I came here to make money for you. We saw the ad in the paper and I saw the show on Oprah where they touted the jobs and the money and the wealth of opportunities available. I thought maybe they needed a chef or even a carpenter. I could send you money.

◇

I burned a few pages last night. It was colder than usual and I had no spare paper to light my wood scraps. I'd filled it all with words. I crumpled it into tight balls, covered with tiny twigs, tumbleweeds, and then dry branches and logs. I used a single match, I shuffled around the pile to distribute fire. The paper caught and the crumples expanded. I could make out a few words when the glow illuminated the world, but as soon as I recognized them, they turned to ash and floated through the room. Thoughts and memory wasted to carbon, the heat eaten by cold. I don't pray, but I said a prayer, a hope, a wish that you would know or feel the words when they were released to the air. Fire caught the small kindling, I blew into the paper and its edges glowed red and dissolved in the night, more flame bit the wood and warmed my huddled bones.

Every day is a new hope. When I report in the morning, there's an announcement or a rumor or just a feeling that things will change and get better. New food rations, higher pay, computers, a movie house for workers. The grander the promise, the harder the work, the hotter the sun, the more severe the managers when a package arrives a minute late. The promise of the day withers hour after hour, new promises or ideas come and interfere and before long I cannot recall what it was I was so excited about and I am worn out, starved, and only able to move my body to the ration station then to home where I collapse on my mattress.

I started writing down the promises, but then they only taunt me as the day became more and more brutal.

By the end of the day, after checking my motivation for the hundredth time, I would be angrier and more despondent than if I didn't do this. Soon, I had a record of disappointments which left me hollow.

I have learned release hope. I ignore rumors and tune out the announcements. Some people notice my attitude and they ask me if I am okay, why I don't smile and clap when the loudspeaker promises a steak dinner by week's end, or why I don't speculate which movie we might be shown if they re-open the old theater downtown, and isn't it such a lovely old building, like what we had when we were kids. I smile back and I am happy for the hope in their hearts. Their ignorant bliss makes me jealous, their unquestioning devotion lies as far from me as the Man in the Moon.

It lurches in my belly. Is this what pregnancy is like? Is this like when you carried our sweet child, my daughter? I wish this one would die, but I know I'm not feeding it, it's eating me, it builds itself into me in some way. It hollows me and fills me, it has a heartbeat that syncopates with mine. When I lie down at night, the arrhythmic beats thrum chaos and war in my body. It grows through my arms, into my neck, and down my legs. I can feel the strength, but it's a cold-steel resilience, a clammy mechanical force. I don't know how much time I have until it finds a channel into my nervous system, when it takes over my brain. I've noticed my vision shifts. I see more, or different, colors. I see crowds of near-transparent figures wandering the vast desert waste. I don't know what they are, they don't seem human, but aren't distinct enough for me to understand. It's like the old days of rabbit-ear television. A different channel would interfere with what you were watching, or ghost images appeared beside the characters on television.

I suspect someone has given me a drug and that this is all a chemical fantasy, but it persists. LSD wears off. This increases day after day. Maybe I should go into the desert and find peyote or mescaline and trip, maybe that would end all of this, a final flushing purge to reset my mind so that I can concentrate on saving money and coming back home.

I watched Dorsey molt from the inside out. I wasn't able to write for a week. I spent every night taking care of her. I poured water in her throat. She could hardly hold food for longer than a few minutes.

She babbled gibberish. Not fevered mumblings, either. She spoke some other language. Maybe her mind was still in English, but her vocal chords and tongue had changed so that they could no longer make words. Her voice was deep and gutteral, but also musical and resonant. In the course of two days it became like one of those thumping car stereo speakers in a way, each beat was some sort of resounding word I guess. Her eyes pleaded for understanding and I soon noticed their metamorphosis from amber-flecked green beauty to black marbles.

After her eyes changed, the rest was simple finishing touches. Her face became gaunt and frozen; tentacles grew out of her back. They sprouted like seedlings in a forest and in a day grew into the arms of an octopus. One morning her skin had changed from soft and smooth to bumpy and rubbery. What I missed most was her voice and the way she could cut her eyes at me when she was fooling me.

She left. I went to work one day and when I came home, she was gone. She made the bed, the sheet and blanket were perfectly tucked. She'd never done that before. Smooth. Hospital corners. A ray of late-day sun lay across the plane. For her, every morning started with a spring from bed never to look back until it was time to collapse at the end of a day. But on that last day, she'd risen and turned back for a final contemplation and care of our bed, the place of our love and her molting. She smoothed the cover like dirt on a grave. I sleep in the dream of a dead love. I am following her. I will be with her soon. The creep in my throat tells me I don't have long to wait.

✧

Ever since that fool splashed acid in my face, I've grown more angry everyday. I see my face half ravaged by acne and now half-melted and I want to scream. I'd always held hope that the acne and its scars would clear and heal. That's possible, I know it. But now I will never be free of this mask. People tell me I'm lucky that my eye was closed and that I can still see out of both eyes, but their patronage makes me boil with rage. I look at myself and hate what I see then I hate everyone who spasms with revulsion. I know you wouldn't, or I wouldn't care if you did.

I've take out my rage on my body. Despite my wasted state, I push myself farther with push-ups, I lift cinderblocks instead of dumbbells. I will be the strongest man around when I'm done. Already, I'm strong enough to take the food I want from whomever I wish. I realize that humans are so weak.

I can feel power coming back, fury runs through it, forms it. I will make these weaklings pay. Not yet, I still have to avoid trouble, but one day these worms will know what my true will is. I am more than they. I am LaMore.

Philistines

Nolon's head prickled, his skin wrapped cheekbones, his pupils dilated, black discs floated in bloodshot white. Misty's white Irish skin fascinated, he watched single blue vein run her thigh, straight to her crotch. The vein pulsed on the back-and-forth leg, he felt the rest of her veins and arteries dancing, throbbing to the fundamental human rhythm of the heart. The music changed and Misty's hips shimmied and slithered to a fast number. Her body was special, he thought, sweat-slick and rubbery like a snake; her white sweat-licked skin reflected neon signs and he thought that if he stared long enough, if his concentration was specially tuned, he could see himself in her abdomen, his brown face on alabaster. His hands were at his side; she could spin her tits independent of each other, the twirling nipples reflected the eye of God, especially the right one. He couldn't touch, his senses were on overdrive, he felt the stubble on her bald crotch and his ears telescoped to hear her tiny red hairs poking up from follicles, squeezed tight to curl over the pubic bone, hug her labia, spiral at random and delightful angles. Nolon's jaw tightened and his eyes shot laser beams, scanners reading every pore of her body, every nook and cranny of the club, every inch of the whole world. He imagined his penis curling and spiraling up and around her boyish hips, squeezing her small breasts and sliding between her pursed, puffy lips. The new speed made him feel smart, clean and pointed, but also like a lizard, an undulating energy spiraled around his spine to the top of his head. Axle, Misty's bull-dyke girl-friend, had hooked him up. She told him that the stuff was different, it had secrets, she said, it'll tell you if you listen. He glowed with life, God flowed through him, he was infused with the wisdom of the ages. He knew everything, like Solomon, but also nothing, like a godless Buddhist. Nolon was night and day, good and evil, he was the end of the world and the mustard seed that would sprout and save humanity. He would lead his flock to righteousness. He would condemn sinners to the eternal fires of hell. He'd been awake for a few days and Axle's side-winder rocket fuel was gonna get him through Sunday morning; the fat little bag rolled between his fingers. He had twenty-four hours before the sermon. He had lots of work to do.

"You want a private room, preacher?"

"No, not today, Miss Misty." Nolon sucked ice from his glass. "I have to write the Lord's words. Come tomorrow, I have to climb to that pulpit and fly over the congregation, like an angel or a broad-winged Heron. Yes, Heron. Like sweet black Heron I will ease their minds and cure their sorrow, I will change their lives and transform them all into something new, something right. My sweet Melody loves Heron, too, her lovely face breathing sweet air in the room, in our fortress of love. I am full of the holy spirit on this glorious day,

Misty. Where I was feeling down and decrepit, damp as Portland rain, you have lifted me from the gutter like Jesus saving a cripple. Your beautiful ass has inspired me, a full moon hanging plump and ripe to pick, a thing to be howled at and worshipped like the wolfish dog that I am. Your firm little titties opened my eyes, and even though you have no bush to burn, God has spoken to me through your hot snatch. Your perfect sin, skin, and your innocent decay puts a tingle in my nuts which I haven't felt in a few hours, since I left the beautiful Hotel DuMonde."

"I know girls over there."

Nolon wrung his hands, he could hear his teeth grinding, bacteria swam on his nose, building colonies in grease. "I watch the troubled flock. I give the Lord's comfort and the Lord's love to wayward young women. So young and sweet and lovely they are. The Lord loves them, every single one, and he has sent me to work among them, to be as they are, full of sin, yet righteous and a light they can follow to salvation or, regrettably, to an early end, as I saw last night when sweet Dorothy left us after a particularly nasty encounter with a demon from Seattle."

"You sure you don't want a private room? That big black dick wants vanilla. I see it bulge. Whatcha say, preacherman?"

"It's not even 1 o'clock, my dear, there is plenty of time in this fine day. I may revise my position. You know how much I love when you rub over me, moving up and down, so slow." Nolon felt himself engorging, he heard his heart thud. "Fuck it, baby, you know what I need."

Keyed up and high on desire, Nolon watched the stage from afar. He needed to concentrate on Sunday, his sermon to the flock, the Holy Spirit. The girls knew him and saw him writing, struggling with his pen and paper; they knew when to leave him alone, they goddamn well better, he thought. Misty was working new customers. He could see them silhouetted in the bright sunny window, he could fill in the dialogue. He wished he could fuck her, but blue-balls were the point of the hustle: endless desire, no pussy. Besides, even if Misty would bang him, Axle would kick his ass and cut him off from that sweet-ass dope. He fingered the bag. He needed a hit; he couldn't afford to come down. If he let up, he'd sleep for a week.

His eyeballs narrowed to pinpricks, he spotted something, someone new, and he couldn't tear his eyes away. Dope did a lot of things but one thing he could always count on was for it to show him trouble. It kept him safe this way, it told him which whore carried a knife and which needed to be saved. Now, here, he saw the club's oldest dancer, Desiree, in a pantsuit with her hair in a tight bun. She never wore anything but, well, nothing, really. She was with a pale man. She was giving a new girl a hard time for swaying like a corpse on the stage. She must be the new manager or something. The pasty-faced guy was quiet and still like a waxy mannequin or an android from the future. The dark suit was odd for this place, it reminded Nolon of an undertaker; the guy sent a chill down his back. Maybe that old broad will do a better job managing than dancing. His mind went blank for a second and he had a flash, a moment of clarity, and then he knew what the sermon would be about. Philistines. He needed to tell his flock about Philistines.

He sat and motioned to the cocktail waitress for a cheap bourbon. Alcohol was a devil, for sure, but his father had raised him on hellfire, brimstone, and brown liquor. Daddy tried to beat the good lord out of me; Daddy couldn't teach me no good, but he sure filled me with Satan's lies. Every drink Nolon took was for his Daddy and he said a silent toast before tipping each one: may his angry, wretched soul find peace.

Being a Southerner made Nolon an interloper, alien like philistines, but carried the Lord's good word. Being a black man made him exotic, he stood out in every crowd. His mission was pure and righteous; he had the Lord with him, they were joined as one to struggle against evil for all eternity. He would remain forever in the service of his Lord, finding his rightful place in the world, a true servant and humble, asking nothing but giving everything, sacrificing his body and mind for the sake of the mission. He wrote in the notebook, the words flowed, the pen scratched the paper, his handwriting remained typewriter-like and legible despite the rapid-fire of inspiration which poured out in black ink. Philistines were taking over, robbing children of their right to find God, to pray in the schools. Philistines turned Christmas into a celebration of plastic product and diminished the Holy and perfect Word of God himself. Easter was overtaken by false idols; they were making us think we came from apes. He called his flock to rise up against the tide of godless science and technology. Secularism corroded the human spirit. He had no time for punctuation or to reconsider ill-chosen words, no time for anything but white, hot Spirit flowing through him, a beautiful river of peace and salvation. It washed him clean like fire. He ended a thought and looked up.

The little pale guy was looking at him. Nolon felt nails hammer his temples. Left, right, left, right. Each blow drove steel deeper into his brain. The dope talked to him, it was screaming. His brain cracked open. Everything he ever thought, every memory and idea and feeling and notion spilled out like noodles. Nolon's gaze locked on the man, but he tried to stay aware of his world and his place in it. There were too many things to keep track of: the little white guy's focused gaze, the sermon, his children, the speed, Misty's ass shaking across the room, his wife, the Lord, his church, his shiny skeleton, the hotel room where Melody was nodding off, the pecan tree outside of his childhood home. It all was too much to handle and he tried to hold it all but it was like wrestling an octopus and everything inside of him kept spilling out. He returned to reality and the stare still had him pinned him like a frog for dissection. The little guy had black orbs under black bangs, marbles that glinted light, unblinking. Nolon's body and breath pulsed to the tempo of his jackrabbit heartbeat.

He needed to get the fuck out of there. His heart was leaping in his chest, it pulled him up and out of the seat. He put money on the table, enough for the drink. He drained the glass. He felt the vial in his pocket. He still had a two $20-pieces, fat rocks from Worker-Walt on 82nd. He needed to smoke. That. Crack. He loved driving with a head full of rock, it had that certain thing he loved that no other speed could do. Crack cocaine was the king of all the drugs, he thought, it was so tasty, it did for him what nothing else could and that was to give him power, ultimate power. He was He-Man from the after-school cartoons he watched at that white lady's house downtown while his mama worked in the peanut factory. He turned into fucking Superman when those boulders cooked.

Misty stood at the end of the bar; she let him out into the alley; she told him to come back, said that Axle had plenty of powder if he needed it. He'd need it, enough could never make it through the night, more was what he'd need. Crack was king, but Axle's dope was built for marathons. He felt his bag of speed; extrasensory tendrils counted the grains. He'd never get through writing the sermon, much less delivering it, counting the money, spending the money, kissing the babies and their mamas, shaking hands with the men and laughing the Lord's laugh, that deep throated retort that spoke of confidence and dominance.

The alley-air was full of atomized rain, blinding

sunshine, and the smell of garbage. His eyes felt like bruises; he found sunglasses in his suit-coat pocket. Relief.

The pipe.

The vial.

The torch and crackle.

His lungs filled with power, his nuts tingled. He wanted a hole, a whore. He heard moaning. Fucking crack fucking shit fucking with me, he thought. More moans. Louder. A hard-on rose and he wanted to bang the moan but he didn't know where it was coming from. There was a break in the curtain and he could see in the room. It was the nasty old stripper broad bent over a desk. Her floppy tits pressed it. That's a nice desk, he thought. Behind her was that weird-ass guy, getting her good. He was still, his chalky face had no expression and Desi's face was red, her lips a crimson 'O,' her eyes clenched shut. The wormy guy was still in that damn suit, yet she was butt-ass naked and getting off like a champion fucker, a world-class hooker. Nolon never liked her old body, but she emanated pure ecstasy and her body sang to his. He'd let that blonde bitch suck it, he guessed, her mouth never looked diseased. He pulled out his cock and stroked it. Desi looked better and better with each pull and soon he felt warmth rise through his body. He was going to come. He wanted to put it on her face or tits. He started to ejaculate, his eyes clenched shut. When looked up again, the little guy was staring at him. The nails came back to his temples, he heard a scream deep in the center of his lizard brain. He was still coming, the golden wave of pleasure crashed headlong into a deep, animal fear, he knew a pain he never imagined possible. He lost total control and cried out from the center of suffering, releasing something between a cry of pain and an animal howl. Desi's echoed scream was pure mirth and freedom until her eyes popped open, met his; her face contorted, the rosy glow of passion turned into a crimson rage. Nolon pulled his pants up, buttoned the top and made off down the alley. His cock, half-hard and dribbling, fell out, he shoved it back in and kept going, walk-running, he wrangled with the zipper.

Nolon lit a cigarette, the car cranked. He loved the roar and purr of the V-8. He mashed the gas, spun the tires, and the car bounded into traffic bouncing sideways, squealing where the parking lot met the road. Rotted windshield wipers left steaks in the window, turning strips of the city into blurry arcs, indecipherable parts which he could only guess about, slices of urban landscape warped to a watery dream as he raced down streets and avenues, boulevards and alleys. There was nothing in the rear-view but he sprinted from red light to red light, putting as much distance between himself and the club as he could. Just drive, he thought, get away. That little guy's eyes sent waves of fear through him. What kinda guy looks like that, he wondered, nobody has black crow's eyes, so dark you couldn't tell what he was looking at. Who can fuck a woman so that she howls like that, yet not even move? Who would ever fuck Desi, anyway? Shit was seriously askew, he thought. That guy must not know better. He'd seen some wormy-looking guys before, but not like him. The key was the eyes, those black, unblinking spheres, and that scream-ing, blinding pain in his head. None of it made any god-damn sense. Before, in the club, the guy seemed to sift through his brain, looking for something. There must be more like that guy, he wasn't one of the Lord's mistakes, he was a new race, an invading species.

Nolon felt nauseated, raw, and used. He felt he'd been molested by an uncle or scraped out like a melon. Bile crawled his esophagus to the back of his mouth. He turned off the main road and choked down the acid. He knew he was being followed, he knew it wasn't over. Deep in his God-fearing soul he heard a voice call out to fight the pale guy and his friends. A holy war, a sacred spiritual struggle. Maybe all the dope was play-ing tricks with his mind, it was hard to tell; he wanted another hit. He had Axle's killer dope in his pocket and he tried to calculate the grains, each a strong and silent soldier that would wrap his brain as tight as a Christ-mas present under a sparkly fir tree. With one hand, he loaded the pipe for another hit, a gallon of gas to throw on the red-hot coals of Axle's dope. He took the hit. Crack exploded in an exciting, erotic way that shot him through with power and energy. The world warped, muted colors in the Portland day came to life, and a hard, glossy sheen coated everything; it was as though the world had iced over and had the sort of beauty that forbids you to touch, so that you never know if it exists outside of your own mind. The town was a crystalline jungle, a frosted city that promised to never melt as long as Nolon kept his contract with the Father, the Son, and the Holy Ghost. Amen.

He lit another cigarette. He snapped back into time. He didn't know where he was. He was lost in a labyrinth of bungalows where pitted concrete streets stopped and started at a whim, the grid broke at random intervals and he ground his teeth. Portland had him trapped, each turn created more confusion. How do I get back to Powell, where is Division? Where the fuck am I? The more he tried to leave the residential area, the more the roads constricted and confined him, strangling his movements and tightening on his chest, a big fat snake that never let go. He'd passed the same yellow house five times, or was that a different one? His throat tightened. He lit a cigarette. Didn't I just light a cigarette? Time fast-forwarded then dropped to slo-mo, he checked the rearview mirror. Nothing. Did someone just jump behind a car? The dashboard was a squishy sponge, the car was a boat, bobbing on uncertain seas. A nearly-whole cigarette burned in the ashtray – where the fuck did that come from? The rain increased, coated the windshield, the wipers slapped and banged; rivers of water arced over the window.

He found the main road and released a sigh. He must've lost anyone who was following, he thought. Everything was smooth and he made it to the hotel alongside the tracks, a flop for sailors and dockworkers on shore leave. The full-timers were all scared, lonely, and desperate souls who needed to hide from something that wouldn't leave them alone. The clerk took cash and never asked questions.

The parking lot was full of old cars with oxidizing paint, broken tail lights, and questionable ownership. Melody was awake and smoking when he walked in the room. The curtains were open, she sat in a pool of sunlight; her brown eyes gleamed. Her black bra and panties glared contrast against alabaster skin. The heat was on full. She looked up at Nolon and bounced on the bed like a little girl. High as a fucking kite. She passed a pink rubber ball from hand to hand, giggling and bouncing, when she tossed it over her head she broke out into a peal of girlish laughter.

"I scored some incredible dope, baby. "She sat, her face beamed like that of a 10-year-old girl." Nolon smiled at her innocence and cherub-like cheeks. When he blinked he saw a haggard old woman, a soul had been worn down with life and weather, drugs, and time. He rubbed his eyes, took a deep breath to find the 25 year-old junkie miles from home and with no cares in the world.

"This is serious, child. We gotta keep these fucking windows closed." Nolon snapped the drapes shut. He peeked out, his eyes scanning every inch of parking lot, under every car. They were everywhere. He saw about five of those little pale guys hiding behind the scrub tree in the parking lot, two peeked from behind the ice machine at the adjacent building, and three more were lying under cars. Fucking cowardly devils, come out and face me.

"They're something more, something worse. I know there are more of them. Fuckers. They are seeping through the cracks. Acid rain through a leaky roof." Nolon peeked out the window. "Why won't those motherfuckers show themselves? Why can't they goddamn come out. We gotta keep an eye out, baby. Keep the drapes pulled and watch out."

"They won't hurt us." Melody tossed the ball and when it bounced on the ceiling she broke into a fit of hysterics.

Nolon rifled through his pockets, producing the vial of rocks, his pipe, and the torch. The rock glowed a beautiful orange and his lungs puffed with power, his heart raced with love. That fucking bitch had stepped out on him while he was across town working on his sermon.

"I got some new shit," Nolon said. "I must not sleep, if I do I might not wake up to give my sermon. I must not... Hey, how the fuck did you get dope? You ain't got any money."

"Guy gave it to me."

"Dope fairy?" Nolon stared at her hard.

"Something like that." Melody looked away.

"You filthy, sinful bitch."

"You're a sinner, too."

"Repent, whore." Nolon's nostrils flared, he felt a bull rising in him. "What have we been talking about?"

Nolon's face softened to his caring-conselor face. "You must do as I say, child. You know this."

"How can I get more if I'm fucked up?"

"You let me handle that," Nolon cracked his knuckles. "Sit still, sit up straight. Hands at your side. You know how this goes. Your ass'll still work, you'll still get your dope. A face ain't the only thing in the world. Stay still, don't scream, everything will be okay."

He tilted her chin up so that a sliver of light through the closed curtains caught her green eye, yellow flecks shimmered. Nolon pressed his lips to her lips, he eased into them as into a warm, clean bed. He held his breath and kissed her forehead. He took a moment to take off his rings, he wasn't a brute. He cocked his shoulder.

He began.

His fist hardened and his heart swelled with pity and burst with love each time he dealt a blow to her face. When blood mixed with tears and thinned into watery pink, he stopped. He hated having to do it, but she needed discipline. The Lord said to never spare the rod and he did what the Lord wanted. It was God's will that she learn and his burden was to teach and help her to grow in the light of God. She was a whore and whores only fuck for money. He held her in his arms and kissed her head, whispering to her how he loved her, how beautiful she was, how any whore who was with him better fuck for money or else only fuck him because his big black cock brought her closer to redemption. She sobbed soft understanding and when his shirt soaked with bloody tears he took it off. Melody rubbed his belly. Her fingers went under his waistband.

"Do you forgive me, Nolon?"

Nolon murmured and pushed her hand into his pants. "Go wash yourself. Come back and suck my cock."

He took hits on the pipe. Her mouth took all of him. Melody was the only one who could do that and he loved her for it. Even if she was a filthy whore, she made him feel like a man, something his wife never could do. Fuck. How long had it been since he called his wife? The drapes moved and his body stiffened. He wanted a gun. He pushed Melody off his dick and pointed at the window.

"Those fuckers, they're out there, baby."

"Can you fuck me now?"

"Look at the drapes. Something is back there. Watch those shadows move."

"The air came on, baby." Melody lay back and pulled her pants off. She rubbed herself and moaned. "Give it to me. I want it, baby."

"We're being watched, I can't stay hard with those fuckers out there." Nolon got out of bed and paced the room. "What the fuck are we gonna do? We're fucking trapped." Melody rubbed herself more and writhed on the bed, she moaned, she swirled the bedsheets with her legs and free arm. Nolon stopped pacing and watched her. His endless need for sex fought his fear and paranoia. The men waited for him. Her pussy gaped and bobbed up and down. His dick started to rise. He held it in his hand and stroked it once before sliding between her legs and entering her with a swift, gliding press of hips. She was wetter than ever and let loose a scream of ecstasy that pierced his ear and excited his pelvis. He pounded her with his love.

"Give me a cigarette, baby," Nolon reached for the television remote. "I gotta get my mind off these guys."

"Oprah's on."

She didn't look him in the eye when she handed him a cigarette. He hated when she did that, he thought she was hiding something. He smoked and flipped channels. He found a show about snakes. Their bodies and deadly speed entranced him. He watched a constrictor wrap itself around a rabbit, squeezing life from it and devouring the body. Was a snake anything more than a muscle with an appetite? He thought of the serpent in Genesis, the Great Deceiver. His breath pressed out, his chest tightened and squeezed his lungs. He transfixed on the snake and the innocent rabbit, the cruel cycle of life. Humans were above all of that, the top of the food chain. Yet there were snakes among us, humans serving a darker spirit, individuals fixated on pressing out the life of God and the spirit of salvation.

What was the relationship between the Philistines and Satan? Both tried to press the Lord's word out of schools and out of the great institutions of the United States. They sought to persecute the Lord's people, the chosen ones were forsaken according to them. The Lord sent his son to bring us to truth and away from deception. What were these pale men? Where had they come from? He had to find out more. He had to expose this. It was his duty to serve, to shine the light of truth into the darkness of lies. He felt a rising in his chest and he reached for the pipe. He only had a few shards of crack left. He needed more. He smoked what he had and rode the wave of righteousness he felt rising in his heart, a swell of truth and strength and light to open the minds and hearts of his congregation.

"Hand me that pad of paper, baby."

"You put on Oprah?"

"Give me the fucking paper!"

Melody got off the bed and retrieved his notebook from his rumpled coat on the hotel table. He found the channel with Oprah. Melody nestled beside him.

Oprah's guest, a young blonde woman, a journalist, was talking about how everyone was out of work and how great it was that people were able to get jobs with some company that had been taking over and revitalizing – the word was *revitalize* – small towns in budgetary distress. The young woman was a bubbly investigative reporter full of enthusiasm for the company she'd been investigating. It was like she was talking about a charity or a benevolent person. Nolon lit a cigarette and found the brown liquor he'd lain under the bed that morning. Oprah looked especially hot, he thought. He took a long pull on the bottle. Oprah's diet must be working for her, Steadman was a lucky son-of-a-bitch these days. She knew how to purge but, full of sin, always returned to corpulence, indulged her flesh and willful ego. Still, for now, he would like to fuck her. Oprah took questions from the audience. A man from Idaho wanted to know how he could get in touch with the company and find a job. His wife clapped and cried. A girl from Indiana was curious about the woman's gorgeous golden tresses. The audience laughed. Oprah bounced around the audience, shoving the mic in the face of Americans brimming with curiosity and the excitement of opportunity. Nolon took a deep swallow from the bottle. He dipped a fingernail into Axle's speed. He snorted the drug and his brain lit up like a pinball machine. The audience members took on a surreal quality, amorphous blobs that snapped back to solid, Oprah changed from devil to angel and back. Fear gripped his chest but his dick was rock hard. He was staring into the gaping maw of a bulbous human with a Minnesotan accent when his focus shifted to the reactions of the audience.

Three rows back, he saw another man just like the one in the club. Black eyes, black suit, pale skin and a stony face. The eyes focused into the camera, directly at Nolon, unblinking marbles pounded his chest through the cathode ray tube of the hotel television and his breath left him, carried off in waves of panic and terror.

"There!" Gasping, hyperventilated, panicked.

"Wha?" Melody was cooking dope, loading a needle.

"Look, look – there it is," Nolon said, he shook his finger at the television, struggled for air. "It's one of them men that I been talking about!"

"Where, baby?" Oprah's face filled the screen and thanked her sponsors with cheeks aglow and teeth gleaming. "Oprah's cool."

"Shit, you missed it." Nolon heaved, regaining composure. "It was him, or it was one of them. It was just like that fucker I saw at the club. He was looking at me, too. He knew I was watching him. That fucker looked right through me, that little beast knows I know. I think I'm figuring this shit out, baby. This shit is huge. Forget how socialism is destroying our nation, or whores and homosexuals teaching our children. This is bigger than all of that. All of that is Satan's distraction from what's really going on, he fools us with minor worries that divide us. This could be the end of us all, baby, an unholy end at the hand of these devils. I feel it in my bones."

"This is what you're like when you're jacked." She patted her ankle to raise a vein.

"You've never seen one of these fucks, they know what you're thinking, they crack open your skull and they can tell if you're watching them."

"*Pfft*. That shit was filmed weeks ago. It's not live, Nolon." Melody pressed the plunger nice and slow. A noise like a cat's purr rose from her throat and she melted into the mattress.

"I don't care. He knew I'd be watching. He knew it, even before I did, before you even said you wanted to watch Oprah. Did he tell you to watch Oprah? You never want to watch Oprah. What the hell? Who gave you that dope? What did he look like? Look at you, fucking nodding out when I'm asking you a fucking question. Fucking whore. He seen me, I know it as sure as I know my own name, as a God-fearing sinner and humble servant, I know he knows and I'm starting to think you know. You wanted to watch, you made me put it on and see him and he saw me and now he knows what my prick looks like, all limp and helpless. If he knows I bet all of them know, too. I bet they're on the way to this motel right now and we're all fucked all to hell, Melody. Damnit bitch." Melody's mouth hung open, her lip dribbled drool, she soared on a cloud of Heroin and forgotten dreams.

Nolon sat, paralyzed. Fear, blind panic set in with the twist of speed and uncounted days of no sleep; his chest felt like it would explode. He waited for the men to show back up and stare him down. He fixated on the image of that man in the audience, the still, chalky face standing out amongst the pink cheeks, chocolate noses, and fake-tans in Oprah's regular studio audience. How in the hell did he get in there? He must have been planted by Oprah or one of her staff. The show was filmed in Chicago, he knew this, he'd gone to Bible College on the North Side years ago. She was just starting out then and there were dorm-room debates as to whether or not she was on the side of the Lord. He still didn't know, and his doubt mounted. She never said much about the Lord, like how atheists say good things but never call out Jesus' name. Oprah was powerful and if these pale guys had gotten to her, the country was in certain jeopardy. This could be world-wide. Her empire

existed on a global scale, her fingers extended wherever they wanted to go. There were in things Oprah
herself probably didn't even understand. All she did
was watch numbers come in. Minions reported half-
truths and soothed her with revenue increases. Nolon
floated into a daydream of paranoia, he postulated her
in cahoots with a global underground of aliens and elite
bankers, illuminati and dark priests. His mind ran out of
steam, he started, his body shaken and shocked. He was
watching a rerun of *Busom Buddies*. He looked around
the room for his satchel; he needed protection.

His gun was in his bag under the bed. Nothing gave
him a feeling of power quite like a .45 revolver. Dirty
Harry, motherfucker.

Nolon twirled the cylinder, he bounced gun-heft
from hand-to-hand. He sat at the table and cut a powder
trail on the mirror. He ripped into it with a snort and he
was knocked into a vortex of muted color, like one of
those old-timey novelty lollipops, spinning and bitter, a
savory tang that sat on the edge of his mouth, tempting
him to chase it in hopes that it would taste better, that
he could get more of the flavor. The blast clarified his
mind, twisted his perceptions to focus in a way that he
could not fully comprehend, a dancing sort of understanding which existed at the periphery of consciousness. He felt light, as though he were falling and his
stomach was rising into his chest. Then he heard something from far off, an echoing sound, a voice that rum-
bled thunder. The voice entered him, a divine posses-
sion; he listened to it and it told him truths he'd sensed

but could never vocalize, revelations which scared him but now were made real. Some rough angel had taken his body, jaw, and throat, and it spoke through him.

The voice said: "I know the answers, I know it all. It's coming into focus. There is a group, devils who have come in bad faith. They look like men, but they are not men, they are some sort of other race, an animal or alien or other beast unknown, a species intent on sucking the light from human life. They are here on Earth, or maybe from the bowels of the Earth, little is known of their origins. They are here for our riches, for the bounty of Earth and they need humans to make their dreams a reality, they will be our masters, we their slaves and they will feed upon us, as lambs fatted for a feast. They corrupt those they can corrupt, dupe and enslave others, more will be resistant to them and they will seek to destroy us. We are diverse, more diverse than we even know. A select few, Nolon, will see the truth of it all. This select group must find one another and speak the truth, must liberate the slaves, as Moses freed the Jews of Egypt. This group is the only hope for humanity, the only ones to pave a road to the future and to lead us all to a new era in God's grace and bounty."

Nolon shook himself. He awakened. He grabbed the notebook and sat at the table, transcribing what he'd heard. The Word of God had sprouted from his mouth. A new chapter of the Bible was being written, by and about him. He always knew he was special. That was what kept him sane all those times his father had whipped him, his mother's soothing refrain that he was a special boy meant to do great things and that his father loved him and was trying to teach him a lesson of humility and strength. It was now coming true, he was the vessel of the Father, a prophet chosen to lead His people from slave drivers, to lead an uprising of the righteous and the saved. He wrote down everything the voice said. He wrote down everything that had happened in his life. He wrote the mythology of himself, a text that would explain to everyone why things were as they were, why it was his purpose to lead them all. Historians would thank him once he thwarted the evildoers, once he had led the chosen ones to a new tomorrow, free of oppression, free to bask in heavenly light and peace.

Nolon's story was epic, heroic, archetypal. On the night he was born there was a hurricane which had blown up from the Gulf of Mexico to the flatlands of South Georgia, the windows shook and the room was lit with a lantern and lightning. Nolon painted the picture: His grandmother coached his mother through the birth with shadows dancing on the walls, the crags in his grandmother's face; his father was playing dice in the next town. The storm was at its peak when his mother pushed him into the world. The baby Nolon bursting from darkness into a dim yellow glow, glistening with the wet of the womb. At the moment of his screaming birth, lightning struck a century-old pecan tree outside, his first sound in harmony with the booming crack of electricity and wood. The trunk was stripped of bark in a spiral all the way to the ground, a scar remains in that tree to this day. That was Nolon's scar. It wasn't enough for the vessel of the Lord to have the trauma of birth, his arrival on Earth left a marker, a living monument for all of God's creatures to see.

In school, white kids persecuted him for being black and the black kids punished him for following Jesus, for being too white. His skin was always ashy, his hair was nappy, and he wore a suit every day, washing the shirt by hand at night and wearing it wet, the morning sun dried it while he fed his hogs and milked his goat. He didn't father a child until he completed seminary and was an associate pastor. The kids he grew up with had multiple children by their 20th birthday. He was later tested by drugs and crime, the Almighty's trial taught him a decrepit life. He crawled among the lowest in society, yet held strong to faith. Like Jesus, he consorted with whores, thieves, villains. He embraced the meekest of the earth and was inspired by their beauty and grace. He would lead them from slavery, he would take them to a new tomorrow full of God's love.

He filled twenty pages in tiny, typewriter handwriting, each letter crafted, each word chosen with high-pressure amphetamine exactitude. The words images, his thoughts mechanical parts driving him forward, each a cog pushing against the other cog, spinning axles, creating momentum. He was a fucking genius. The words proved his worthiness as a leader and visionary. Philistines were a reality in life, interlopers to God's holy property. Would anyone dare to allow a sinner to run his house? Should a church be run by secularists? Of course not, he wrote, it was a simple logic and God's plan was a simple one. There were holy, spiritual people one one hand, and on the other hand were the sinners, the interlopers, Philistines who were jealous and hateful of the holy, who would stop at nothing to foil the progress of the Christian soldier. It was just that simple.

There were voices. Nolon dropped to the floor. Fuckers are out there, he thought, looking for me, trying to get me. He crawled across the floor to where he'd left the crack pipe and the vial. One left. Fuck, he was gonna have to leave to get more. He checked his cellphone. It was five o'clock. Five o'clock rock, here it comes, here comes the fucking rapture. Boldered, fucking killed, the rock's power ran through him and he wanted more. He crawled back to the table, to the bag of speed. Whispers sprouted up all around. Murmurs moaned in the walls and door. Shadows played against the walls, under the door, in his mind they danced and mocked him, telling him that he would die, that he was a fool to believe in God. Melody snorted in her nodding sleep and he jumped a foot in the air. He pressed himself to the floor and sent an arm up to the table, periscoping a hand to feel for the mirror, the blade, the straw, and the bag of pure white goodness that would rocket a crackhead into the 4th dimension.

Pressed flat, the table shadowed him, he cut a line and admired his face in the mirror. More noises came from outside, murmurs and whispers, he thought he heard someone put a bullet in the chamber of a nickel-plated .45 automatic, that was the image in his mind. Chop the powder. Listen. Chop. Listen.

Don't breathe.
Chop. Listen.
Don't.
Breathe.

Shape the powder into a line, geometric symmetry. Cut the line into two lines. Cut the two lines into four lines, skinny cuts on the vertical axis. Make each line as straight as the edge of daddy's razor strop. He used to untie it from the bathroom door, a face full of lather. He'd grab by the handle and make you drop your drawers. It cut flesh and left whelts on the back, legs, neck. The white lines were a perfect parallel, no grains or dust sullied the mirror. Two for each nostril. One for the good. One for the evil. One for the money. One for the show. Go cat, go!

His eyes watered and his nose felt like he'd plugged it into the wall. His body was fluid. His brain was fire. The speed was doing things to him no other drug had ever done. He closed his eyes to savor the euphoric rush. The murmurs and whispers became a din of noise, every conversation in all of Portland buzzed and chattered at once, a white noise of voices. As soon as he thought he could hear a single voice, he'd lose concentration and would think he was hearing another. He heard voices of pain, joy, sex, dying. The human orchestra played a private concert for him, full volume.

He was in the middle, he knew, he could conduct the players if they would listen to him. When they saw him there in the center with the knowledge and power they needed, they would all listen and follow and be saved.

He opened his eyes. The carpet threads grew into tentacles. They swayed and waved as in an undersea current. They grew faster than kudzu. Nolon watched, transfixed, forgetting all trouble and tormentors. The carpet fibers were talking to him, trying to tell him something. He couldn't decipher the vision, he was locked in its trance, a new rising panic bubbling from within. The tentacles expanded and contracted, waving back and forth. A large, ropy, muscular tentacle jumped from the floor and grabbed his right arm, then his left, he couldn't escape. They were too strong. They had his legs, too. His sternum pressed into the hard floor, he could feel concrete under the thin carpet. He whimpered for his life. He asked God for forgiveness, he knew he was going to die. He prayed.

"Dear sweet and merciful Jesus, I have been such a sinner, I have done so many bad things in my wretched human life. I have lain with whores, I have taken strong drink, drugs, I have abandoned my wife and children. But it has all been for you, my savior. I have tried to follow you, consorting with the meek, the worst of us, the lowest humanity can offer, so that I might help them and save them and pass your word to them. I have kept my church, yes Lord, and, though they are unaware, I have betrayed them all. Yet, their money goes to this mission work, this love and work I have built. The tentacles around his arms tightened. Dear Lord, sweet Jesus, please come to my aid, these creatures are threatening to destroy all of humanity. The Bible showed us the threat of the interloper, the nonbeliever, those who would carry us away from your word and your love. Now I see, now I know what they want. They will imprison us all, they will tear us asunder and bring us to our knees; their aim is nothing short of domination over this world your father, our God, made for us. Please help me now, Lord, help me to live so that I can fight as your soldier, my head at your breast, my sword held high. If you can save me, Jesus, I can complete my sermon and I can tell the truth to my people and we will start the fight in your name."

"Who the fuck are you talking to?" Melody threw the words from a half-sleep stupor.

Nolon snapped to reality. The tentacles vanished, the carpet returned to dingy, thin, puke-green shag. He was on the floor. He was alive. Had he been saved? Had his prayer been answered? He rested his ear to the ground and listened. Nothing. No sound but the thrum of the heater. No one was in the room but he and Melody. He raised up to see Melody nodded, dosed on that good smack. He licked residue from the mirror. One more line.

"Hey baby, you got more of that shit?" Melody's voice blurred.

Nolon fingered the bag. Not much left. Where the hell had it all gone? Fuck. He'd have to call Axle.

"If you keep your goddamn legs shut until I get back, I'll get you high."

He dumped the rest of the bag and cut out four lines. Two fat, two skinny. He'd need more, finding Axle might take time. Melody wasn't into speed, she wanted something to keep her awake so she could enjoy the heroin.

"Bring that preacher cock back."

The parking lot seemed safe. He saw men creeping in the shadows, hiding behind bushes, but Nolon had the protection of the Lord, so he was not afraid. The fresh and fickle speed building confidence, boosting him to do a deal with Axle. It was a tricky mistress, this new speed. In an instant, it could make him feel like a turd at the bottom of the world. The next second he'd be a superman. He straightened his rumpled, torn suit jacket; he pushed his spine to erect, but it lost its posture. He shaped his dry and nappy hair. He was the perfect picture of a junkie. He straggled sideways, he twirled around to catch figures in the shadows, he laughed to himself. He gathered his composure, thrust his nose up to the heavens, proud, a decent man on a righteous mission. The sun was falling, the sky darkened. Mist stuck in his three-day beard.

The car was cool and quiet. Rain clattered on the roof, the windshield a sheet of water. Nolon fumbled for his phone. It was never in the same pocket twice in a row. He pressed the button to call Axle, the speed sharpened his teeth. He hoped he'd be able to see Misty, even if he couldn't touch her. The phone rang, each tone a dilated torture device. The silence between tones was an empty eternity.

"Preacher?"

"Is there more?"

"I'm busy, man."

"C'mon, I need more," he tore open a flattened pack and pulled a bent cigarette out. "I can meet you wherever you need." He held the flame under his chin. It lit.

"Busy."

"What the fuck?" Nolon pulled smoke deep into his lungs, the crumpled arc dangled between his lips, bobbling with his words, "I need that fucking shit, I can't get it out on 82nd."

"Look, I can't help you." There were strange murmurings, hissing noises, an organic white noise filled the background. "Yes, okay. I'm going to text you the address of someone who can help. Misty'll be there soon, too."

"Where? I need the shit! I got shit to do!" Silence. "Hello? Hello? Fuck!" The phone bleated in his ear. An address. A house in Northeast Portland, a decent neighborhood for drugs and hookers who'd cut you as soon as look at you. Another message had instructions to ask for someone named LaMore; to say Axle sent him. Nolon's hand trembled, his nerves jangling from days lacking sleep and regular doses of cocaine and amphetamine. It took a few tries to get the key into the ignition switch. Thank God the car still starts.

There was a break in the clouds over downtown and the sunset burned a swath of deep red against the black, white, and grey gauze. Nolon took his eye from the expressway and stared into the open wound in the sky. The sky is crying, he thought, it's been cut deep by the injustice on this Earth. This is a sign, a holy writ from God: the interlopers are harming the sanctity of the earth and its people, the time to act was now, before all of humanity falls to the corrosion of these Philistines, aliens, evildoers who will cut us open and we bleed like the sky's wound.

He didn't know how they were doing it, not exactly, but he was sure he knew *that* they were doing it, they were trying to take over the world, trying to take truth from the Earth and supplant it with lies and fear. His sermon would show the truth, he was certain, it would be a powerful oratory which would move people to action.

Traffic was light on the highway and he thought he could keep on going up to Washington, find his wife and kids up in Olympia or Port Angeles, he forgot where they were. He'd have to tell them, he had a duty to save them, too, just as he did to save everyone. Maybe he could go find them after church tomorrow. They'd be so glad to see him, he was certain, his daughter would want to sit on his lap and his son would want to play football on the video game unless the weather cleared enough to throw a ball in the yard.

He got off at Lombard. He could feel the memory of powder going in his nose. He knew the street, he knew the best route to getting there because it cut off at John St, but picked back up later at Rose Ave. There were so many dope houses up here that he had the entire area memorized.

He sat in his car and stared at the property. This was a drug house, but there was no moss on the roof, the lawn was mown and the edges were clean. He felt a feeling of home and domesticity, a sense of ease and welcome that he had forgotten and was longing for. An easy acceptance, a place where he didn't have to dole out discipline or drugs in order to have love, where there was no danger and life was simple. Sweetness like chocolate cake and iced tea on a hot day. A liquid flow in a life full of smiles and achievement.

He rolled the window down and took a deep breath and he held it for a moment, then sipped in more air and held that. The air was cool and mist coated his face. He thought he was going to pop like a balloon but he held the breath longer. Finally, he released it all in a gush and felt lightheaded but a little bit at ease, soothing chemicals flowed inside of him. His body tingled and he felt a little high. He'd have to remember this trick later once he took a new hit.

"Yeah"

"Axle sent me," Nolon rocked on his feet, tried to keep cool, calm. "LaMore here? I'm looking for LaMore."

The door opened onto a nice entryway. Moans and screams came from other rooms, the sounds hard to place. The door slammed behind him and a nervous-looking man stood there in his underwear then pointed down the hall, so Nolon started walking. He peeked into the living room and saw a couple on the floor clawing at one another, another couple was on the sofa, the girls howled. Nolon nodded to himself, an approval. He would like this place. He continued down the hall, figuring LaMore would make himself evident.

"You that preacher Axe told me about?" A man with a grizzled, half-burned and half-pockmarked face stared him in the eyes. He was shaving hair from a stubbly beard with a large hunting knife. He wore a tank top undershirt, covering a taut torso, highlighting his muscled right arm. A black rubber glove went up over his left bicep.

"Yeah, I need some of that good dope you got," Nolon said. He could see dried blood on the hilt of the knife. "A full eight-ball, I got the cash. You're LaMore, right?"

"The fuck you think? Sit in the living room. I'll be right with you."

Nolon sat in a chair in the living room. A large fire blazed in the fireplace and a young, naked woman squatted and poked the fire. Nolon's high was raging. Hallucinatory images of the girl as a Neanderthal, stoking a primordial fire, flashed in his mind. She didn't speak or look around, she fixated on the fire and didn't respond when he called to her, if his words had even been audible. He was not sure. Her ribs cast shadows, her eyes were hollow and her hair was stringy-greasy-thin. He grew an erection listening to the couples who fucked on the floor. He watched one girl, a blonde, on her knees and moaning. She was beautiful until she stopped writhing and Nolon saw her skeletal face, a pair of feeble, malnourished breasts swung, each like a pool ball in a sock. He turned back to the girl at the fire. She was looking at him with a doleful look, a Dickensian waif in need of a fix and a good fuck. Please, let me have another.

"Preacher, give me two-hundred."

Nolon found his wallet and his last two hundred-dollar bills. I get a collection plate tomorrow.

"Here ya go."

"Say, preacher, you wanna stick around and fuck some of these girls?" LaMore rested a hand on the hilt of his knife. "There are some more in the back and I think Axle's girl is coming here soon, too. Axle won't be back for a while." He winked and gold teeth glinted in his mouth.

"This fire is fucking hot."

"Hey, Preacher, come back with me We need to get to know each other." The knife creaked in its scabbard as LaMore rested his gloved hand on it.

Nolon followed him back down a long corridor, past numerous bedrooms, each with a couple or two fucking with the door open. The house seeming to expand before him like Alice in Wonderland, he thought, an endless kaleidoscope of sex and drugs. He wanted to save the poor lost souls, one cracked-out girl at a time.

"Here, light this," LaMore made himself comfortable in a large master bedroom. Nolon took a lighter to the joint, fired it up, and inhaled. The smoke soothed his jangly nerves. He passed to LaMore.

"How many people in your congregation, Preach?"

"I think about five hundred, only about a hundred or so show up regular."

"Good smoke, huh?"

"Doing me right."

"They all black folks, like you?"

"Mixed. I ain't like those Southern black preachers, but I ain't exactly stiff like a lotta white preachers. Plus, I have the best choir in the whole Pacific Northwest."

"They love you?"

"Every goddamn one," Nolon's voice squeaked to hold the cannabis smoke.

"I had a preacher when I was a kid, he liked to touch us," LaMore took a deep draw on the joint. "He made me and my sister touch each other and he touched himself." He adjusted the knife, exhaled, and handed the joint to Nolon.

"Some do abuse their flock," Nolon said, keeping an eye on the knife. "God have mercy on their poor, tortured souls."

"I'd like to cut that son of a bitch," LaMore said, bearing his teeth and laughing.

"I bet you would, LaMore."

"Yup, cut his balls off, feed them to him," he said. "I'd do it, too. I've done it for less. I've done that for fun, just to see what a son-of-a-bitch would do, what his face would look like when I jerked the knife through his nutsack." LaMore grabbed the joint and drew on it. "It's not as funny as you'd think, but I do it every now and then." The leather of the sheath creaked. LaMore reached on top of a dresser and handed Nolon a mirror with a razor. "Cut us a few."

Nolon tapped out for four thick lines worth from the bag. He chopped at it with the razor blade, pulverizing it to fine. Thick lines of perfect, delicious dope. He didn't want that much, but he had to put up a good front for LaMore, he looked at the knife and knew he couldn't hold back. He stared at the glove. The skin at the top looked weird when he moved. It was bumpy and diseased-looking, off-color like it had gangrene or jaundice. Danger oozed from his pockmarks; that knife had seen action. Nolon focused on the dope, the endless white, snowblindness and pure vision. White reflects the full spectrum of light, everything in the world shows up against the white. It delivers reality to us, opens us up for truth and provides the energy and vitality to bring it to fruition. The more he stared at it and chopped it the harder it was to tear himself away, he was mesmerized in the action, yearning for the love he felt when it hit his brain.

"Goddamn, Preacher." The leather creaked.

Nolon divided the pile into two even portions, two sets of two healthy lines. Cellular division, reproduction, the teachers denying God and poisoning young minds with the lie of evolution, the other students wondered if we really had come from the apes. They called Nolon an ape, said his black skin made him less than a man and Nolon despised their evolution which lent their theory an air of credibility. Somehow he and all of those with his skin color had missed the boat to humanity and were still part primate, primal, wild and sub-human. Those fucking kids. Nolon began to get angry, his eyes divided by a line of white on the mirror. He handed the mirror to LaMore who produced a silver straw from a pocket and pulled the powder into his nostrils.

"I love that shit," LaMore's eyes watered. "I just made it. That stuff Axe gave you ain't got shit on this." Nolon snorted his second line. "I'll let you sit in here. You need to be alone for a bit."

LaMore's movement smeared across the room to the door. The slam echoed LaMore's trail passed through it. What the hell was happening? Nolon thought maybe he'd snorted LSD, the colors in the room pulsed from Technicolor-vivid to flat grayscale; a shadow moved around on the floor, it crawled towards his feet, backing off when he threatened it, moving closer again. Figured moved with menace in his periphery. A shadow from the left, it grew out of the carpet and took three-dimensional form, he yelled and it retreated to its place. The one on the right advanced. He saw that he was trapped from the two sides. He could try to jump forward, but the bed was now shimmying in the middle of the floor, a nervous twitch vibrating the bedspread which expanded and contracted, a breathing beast underneath. Icy sweat broke on his brow as he dug hard into his chair, his knuckles glowed white and his eyeballs were fully dilated in blind panic. Was there something trying to push out from under the bedspread? The bed rattled into his jaw which was locked, his teeth creaked against each other. He was trapped, placed in check by ghosts and demons which wanted to kill a Lamb of God. He tried to talk to them, but his mouth was dry and glued shut, his throat was raw and the only noise he managed crawled, like a dying man, up his throat. The sound made it to his tongue, but died before it could vibrate his lips. He was trapped in his body, an observer paralyzed with fear. Maybe it was an effect of the drug, maybe he was dying, maybe he was dead.

The floor whorled, a vortex of muted colors held him in a trance. He watched himself move. The vortex pulled him downwards in a slow-motion, hypnotic freefall. His body moved of its own accord, his mind screamed to be set free, his soul reached for God, Jesus, or someone to help him in this dire moment of paralysis and inertial movement. He watched as his head went over his legs, then to an unobstructed view of the floor, the whirl spun to a point of blackness and he fell in.

At first there was nothing; Nolon floated in a vacuum. The panic waned and he took a deep breath which made him feel good. He saw a field of undersea tentacles, they brushed against his face, arms, legs. A sound of static came to his ear. The static turned into a squeal, then to a piercing shriek, a metallic, industrial noise which he felt in his teeth. He could taste its steel. There was nothing for him to hold onto, he put his hands over his ears, but that was no help. The sound was inside his mind and he screamed for Jesus. *Save me Lord!*

"I am here for you, Nolon."

The screaming in his mind stopped and the tentacles waved. The voice was deep, resonant, and comforting. He looked around himself, he could see his body, naked. He grabbed his arms, legs, penis. He was all there, his heart was beating and his lungs filled with air. It was good.

"Jesus?"

"I am here for you, Nolon."

"Oh sweet Lord, you must help me," Nolon began to cry, he was overwhelmed with emotion. "There are demons on this Earth, they wish to kill each and every one of us. They are Philistines, like in the Bible, but they have more than corruption in mind, I fear."

"I know, Nolon."

"Oh Lord, can you help me?"

"You mustn't be afraid, Nolon," Jesus said. "I am with you, and I am with them."

"Them? But, they are trouble, corrupters, Lord."

"Nolon, your thoughts are confused."

"Yes Lord, but I have saved so many."

"Nolon, you must not fight these men. Their ways are unusual and you will be tested. Soon, though, you will see how much they have to offer, and how richly they can reward all of my followers."

"Yes, Lord."

The tentacles swirled around in a spiral of flashing color like an octopus Nolon had seen on television once. Spiraling, spiraling, he thought, the whirling tumult of life. He was blessed, he was anointed, and he would deliver a sermon to his people that would launch them into a new dimension of holiness. Those who missed it for football or hangovers or to visit relatives would have to be left behind. In his mind he saw the church itself, the wooden, white structure of it, it spun like the tentacles before him, glowing all the colors in the universe, a beacon to God himself, a spaceship hovering upwards to deliver them all to the new holy land, to salvation.

A force pulled his body into the swarming whirl. The ropy arms caressed him and massaged his body; muscles relaxed which he didn't know were tight; he inhaled into lungs he'd forgotten. The tentacles grabbed him, sucked his skin, and pulled his limbs. Ligaments tore and muscles unraveled. He felt himself being torn apart, painlessly, shredded to molecules. His body again found itself, it became solid flesh and bone held together with electricity and hope. The Spirit of Jesus flowed into him. He was shredded all over again, then reconstituted, in a cycle. His consciousness spun inwards, he became dizzy, the amphetamine reemerged in his consciousness, and his body ached from days of chemical tension. His worldly state more fully realized but less believable, less reliable with each turn towards the center.

◇

Carpet fibers mashed Nolon's skin and his eyes felt like they were full of sand, his body ached. He was clothed. He was in a strange room. LaMore. Yes, he was in LaMore's house, the drug dealer who'd sold him a bunch of shit and who got high with him before... Before whatever happened happened. He moved his body and the aches worked themselves out when he rubbed his muscles and stretched. He lay on his back, staring at the ceiling his mind coming to a sharp edge. He pulled himself up and found the mirror. There was residue left, white dust remaining from the lines. He wet his finger and sopped it up then rubbed it on his gums the little bump brightened his mind and body. He pulled up into the chair. A full pack of cigarettes lay on the side table. He wanted to smoke all twenty at once.

The clock beside the bed said 10 o'clock; it was dark outside. Good. Twelve hours until he had to be at the church, thirteen hours until his sermon. He needed to rethink. Things were different, those he thought were philistines were now Jesus' people, a new wave come to save the chosen people, the true believers. He would have to show his flock that they were good, to not fear them, as they surely would without his strength and guidance.

The notebook was in his jacket. He reviewed the sermon he'd written. He'd been so convinced that the world was going to be destroyed by interlopers. He felt so unsafe but now he was going to be at the vanguard of a change so dramatic as to be called a new genesis for mankind.

The door knob turned. Nolon's heart skipped and he gripped the chair's arms with white-knuckle ferocity. The door remained closed and he heard murmurs from the other side. His paranoia returned in full force. He knew he'd be dead in a moment, shot or strangled or flayed with LaMore's knife. The door creaked a bit. He saw darkness on the other side as it cracked. It was moving at a snail's pace but then flew open all at once.

"Hey Preach, what you doing here?" Misty said. She was in a hooded sweatshirt, baggy pants, and had a hat on her head. Off duty, for sure.

"Girl, what the hell you doing?"

"You got dope?"

"Yeah, sure."

He found the baggie and dumped a bit on the mirror.

"More."

"Damn girl."

"I just got off so I'm ready to get off."

"This shit ain't cheap."

"Don't you worry about that, Preacherman."

The powder looked so pure and beautiful on the mirror, like little clouds up in heaven. The razor cut it with ease and in moments each rubbed their nose with red, watery eyes, and a look of dopey bliss on their face.

"That's it, that's it," Misty stood and raised her arms over her head. "I feel like I just won something."

"Take off those baggy pants, I need to see that ass."

"Anything for the Lord, preacher."

"Yes, sister, do it for the Lord."

"You think Jimi Hendrix is in heaven?" The pants fell to the floor.

"All of God's children make it to heaven," Nolon said. "Jimi was blessed with a marvelous talent. I'm sure God has a special plan for him."

"You think he'll come back?" Misty sat on the bed, spread her legs and started rubbing herself.

"I don't know what God has in mind, honey," Nolon stood and dropped his pants, he was fully engorged. He stroked himself. "I sure would love to hear Jimi play. Maybe when we get our reward, we can hear him. Up in heaven."

"With John Lennon?"

"And John Bohnam on drums, raining holy thunder on us all," Nolon said, standing at the side of the bed, pushing himself inside Misty.

"That's it preacher, give it all to me," Misty said, her voice a low purr. "Yes, deep, all the way. Goddamn you're big. All of it, all of it. "

Nolon pressed deep, her lithe body slithered beneath him. He pulled off her shirt, bit her nipple, and slammed himself into her. She moaned and screamed. He felt a rise of energy up his spine to his skull. He slid her across the sheets and remounted her on the mattress. His ear was next to her mouth, he heard her breathe and howl. She started repeating some line in the back of her throat, a chant or prayer or something; he heard indelible sounds in whispery tones patterned like code. He moved in its rhythm, it was hypnotic. He couldn't tell if it was English. Her body clenched around him, her arms and legs wrapped him tight, and he felt himself sucked into her crotch, glued in. He was spinning in space, his body detached from gravity, but whole, and human. He could still do it, his hips continued thrusting and it felt so good, she must have strong muscles, he thought, it's tight like a constrictor.

"Do it Preacher."

"Let me bite that titty."

"Lead us, Preacher." Misty rocked her hips.

"You feel so good, Misty." He jerked his teeth from her nipple and Misty winced.

"Deeper, give it all to me." Her nails dug into his back.

"You got it baby."

"Show the way, Preacher, lead me to salvation," Misty shook her hips. "Make me see the light."

"Flip over."

"Other guys can't come doing all those drugs."

"Blessed, I guess."

"Can you get hard again?"

"Give me a minute, I'll break you in, sister."

"Take us all to heaven, preacher."

"I spoke to the Lord and that's what he said," Nolon heard Jesus' voice in his head and his righteousness swelled. "He said I was the one. Even you Misty, though you are a whore and a sinner, you can follow me and we can join these newcomers. We can show the world how to find salvation, how to release and surrender to God's holy plan. I don't think they will have much choice, but they can be saved if they follow and don't resist. If their willfulness doesn't interfere and they can do what's needed to create the sacred new order of the world, if they surrender their will and become the humble servants of the Lord, they will reap all of his goodness."

"Call me a whore again," she said. "That makes me hot."

"I gotta get out of here." Nolon pulled his pants up.

"Can you give me a ride?"

"Sure."

"It's far, but I'll make it worth your while."

The car was full of a damp chill, the seats were hard and icy. A fresh line of speed brightened things up, warmed the atmosphere, put a zip in the getalong; Misty plugged her music into the radio. Frenetic beats and twirling melodies swam around Nolon's head. Misty turned the volume all the way up and he was in an ocean of sound. He felt young, like when he first found crack and loved the way music and the drug joined to speak a language he would die to hear. The language eroded. Drugs had this effect, he thought, they operated on the law of diminishing returns, your fluency decreases all the time. The first times you speak to them you know exactly what to say and they speak to you in perfect clarity, the words are new and powerful and rich and full of vibrancy. As time moves on, the voice blurs to a noise which only vaguely resembles that first honeymoon fuck, that initial sense of ease and calm becomes more and more elusive, fading to the point where you hardly remember it, where it hardly even matters anymore. All you want is more and you're not even sure why but you do. Then, in moments of clarity, like now, he thought, you remember why you do them, what started it all off in the first place, the payoff you continue to seek. Most things break into an easy comfort, like a hammock or a squeaky pair of new Sunday shoes. Drugs made you less and less comfortable. Ain't that a kick in the teeth?

"Head out 30, Preacher."

"The fuck you want out 30?"

"You wanna get really high?"

Nolon punched the gas and launched them down the twisting off ramp to highway 30. Misty leaned over him in the centrifugal force. Nolon pushed her head back and laughed. Misty giggled. She really giggled like a little girl, or a teenager, a pure clean sound from such a debauched body and mind. Nolon was proud of himself for the moment, for handling the car at such speeds, and playing with her if only to hear that gentle sound. He guessed it'd been years since she giggled like that and would be more years before she would again.

"It's really dark out here."

"Feels like floating in space, like we're no longer on the Earth," Misty said. "Hey turn left up here."

"Light me a cigarette, remind me I'm still a body."

The clouds broke and a full moon shone down on

rolling hills. Nolon craned himself to see up through the windshield, his breath fogged the glass. The sky opened and cleared to a field of black pricked with stars nearly washed out by a full, bulbous moon; the longer he drove the more his eyes adjusted to the dark, his nose chilled from the cool aura of the window; he looked for Orion's Belt, the one memory he had from a college astronomy class, the one pagan entity he could name and pinpoint in every clear black sky. The moon turned the world into a deep blue and white landscape, the mist hanging to fields and mountains was illuminated, an electrified blanket for the Earth. The car dove into a valley and Nolon turned off his headlights and pressed the accelerator. He turned off the music and the car was silent, except for the whine of the engine and wind buffeting the body.

"Yeah, Preacher."

The lines in the road glowed enough to be seen and Nolon's speeded-out eyes telescoped down the road, soaking in every bit of information, every rut and pebble in the road was processed through a jackrabbit, steel-trap mind. He could feel the road, he knew it before it knew itself. He was in control, he was special. He wasn't just saved, he was a leader, a hero, a savior and nothing could ever kill him.

"You're gonna do great, Preach." Misty reached for his crotch and rubbed him. Nolon accelerated.

A curve was coming up, the road appeared to turn and disappear back into the forest. Misty took off her seatbelt and Nolon continued accelerating.

"Whoooo."

"The Lord's got us in his hands, baby, we're right where we're supposed to be." He jammed the accelerator to the floor, the car lurched forward as it downshifted, the engine screamed into his eyeballs, his pores burst open for the thrill of the speed and the darkness ahead.

At the last possible moment, as they entered the moonless dark of the forest, Nolon turned the headlights back on and managed a tight mountain curve; his tires squealed and strained to hold the road, Nolon held the wheel, strong and true, like a true master, a true leader. He turned the big old car into a sleek sportster and he became Mario Andretti, the best racecar driver ever. Misty squealed and grabbed his leg. He thought of those rich white boys in high school who had fast cars and pretty blonde girlfriends. He was like them, but he had God on his side, they only had Daddy's money and racism backing them up.

They slalomed through a tunnel of dark and shadowy trees. Nolon accelerated fast and broke hard into the twisty curves. The car held tight to the road. Nolon's jaw was a locked vice; centrifugal force stressed balding tires through hairpins. He shifted in the seat, leaning into the curves. The car crossed lines, gliding from lane to lane for maximum speed and efficiency, he stayed on the road and never once did the car touch the gravel on the edges of the highway.

"It's up here on the right. Where the trees break," Misty said. "Here!"

Nolon aimed the car off the road between the trees and down a weedy road. It looked like no one had ever driven over the weeds but the path through the trees was clear, a perfect corridor with barely enough room for Nolon's wide-bodied ride. Green hairs slapped the head-lights for a half mile until the trees parted to a wide-open field where a row of identical black sedans parked in a row to the side of a large, Victorian looking house that glowed in the moon's light.

"This is some spread, Misty."

"Yeah, Preach, it's something else."

"You be okay out here?"

"Come in, Preach, Axle'll fill up your supply," she said. "Besides, I think you wanna meet some of our friends out here."

"Kinda freaky out here."

"You're kinda freaky, yourself."

Misty turned and gave him that sexy, pouty-lipped, sultry look which turned him on every single time she did it. He wanted another shot at her, the memory of her body was fresh in his mind. Maybe I can get my real freak on here, he thought. If Axle doesn't kill me for fucking her girlfriend, maybe the three of us... His mind was spinning fantasies faster than he could register them, a blur of image which only registered down in his crotch. He reached to Misty and put his hands in her pants. Wet. He needed no further conversation. Maybe they had a drink of whisky in there.

"You lead the way," Nolon said. "Twitch that ass, girl."

The double door was heavy and thick, a four-inch slab of Douglas Fir dating back over a hundred years. Nolon pulled it open and its momentum almost knocked him over while Misty sauntered into the darkened house.

Inside was a massive hall. Staircases on either side curved up to the second-floor landing. Both sides of the room featured two large fireplaces facing each other with blazing fires; at the far end was a fireplace unlike any Nolon had ever seen. It was five times his home hearth and it was full of blazing wood. Pale men in suits milled around, their shadows long, snaking along a shiny wooden floor. Nolon's skin became electric. He grabbed Misty's arm.

"Who the fuck are these guys?"

"Don't worry, Preacher, these are the ones you need to understand. They're why you're here. Or, you're still here because they let you live." Her eyes looked like deep black pools of oil with glimmering firelight dancing on the surface. A deep, thrumming sound reverberated in his mind, her head seemed to weave back and forth in rhythm, the tones walked down his spine, relaxing him and making him feel more and more at ease. He locked on her beautiful face glowing in yellow-orange light, a Cheshire-cat grin blazed. The sounds drove deeper, polyrhythm liquefied his mind.

"C'mon, Preacher, let's go talk to mama."

Nolon felt numb, but alert, a living brain in a body gone to sleep. He thought a bit about his high, this bender that started when? Wednesday? Monday? It was hard to say, so much had happened. He loved the ups and downs, the tweaked paranoia, the euphoria of getting high and the endless sex. This time he was opened to even newer highs, his relationship with the Lord had been sealed in holy light. Axle's new speed had opened the doors to the divine and his soul was now washed, clean, ready. Now that he had moved to a new plane of existence and it seemed that he was now the foreigner, a stranger in a new world that was welcoming him as a leader, a man to show the way for humanity so they might find peace in this new era of history. In the house, he really was an interloper. He could trust Misty, he knew her, she would be valuable. All heroes needed a guide, a helpmate sent from beyond. It was like the first time he dropped all that acid and his wife had found him by the river, wandering lost. She'd been a guide for him even if she didn't know that he was tripping.

His wife. Karen and the children, Parris and Marika. How far away she was, how ignorant. She could never follow him on this path, this righteous mission. Once he revealed the Lord's new plan she could rejoin him and he could stop using all the drugs and he could live with her and their children again and no one would have to be afraid or insecure or angry or violent or use harsh tones of voice. This had all been a test of their family, they would overcome adversity and be closer, more whole and happy for the rest of their lives. God knew what he was doing all along, it was all part of His plan.

Misty pulled his hand and he floated along with her. He got closer to her and a particular warmth rose from her body, from her crotch. It wanted him. Her vagina was speaking to him, calling for his body. It wanted to latch onto him and suck him inside. It would eat him and he would be eaten just as he wanted to be, as he needed to be. He watched himself from above, in a state of dreamy delirium; Misty held his hand, sure-footed and confident, pulling him like a willing balloon down a darkened flight of stairs.

The long, narrow room was dim-lit and bound by red velvet walls, patterned with whorls and paisleys, the carpet was a deep-pile, black woolen fibers sucked his feet in. Axle was at the far end. She was sitting in a high-backed chair next to a pale man in a matching chair. Nolon hardly recognized her out of her normal blue jeans and boots. She wore a black robe that sank down and disappeared into the carpet. Her mohawk was gone, her head was bald, shiny and clean. She looked like a pagan priestess more than a speed dealer and the guy with her didn't even look human. Nolon's body gripped in fear and anxiety. This was too foreign, he was too far from his regular collection of junkies and the gentle sur-reality of a no-tell motel by the docks. He wondered if he could escape, if he was fast enough to make it out of there without being caught. He could hardly feel his body, but he thought he was in control of it. He could jerk away and dash to the car.

"No," Axle said. "You can't leave, Preacher. You will help us, you will lead the next wave. You must help the world see how we were prophesied, how we are the

Lord's work, the next step as humans evolve towards the divine. Look at Misty, she's proof."

Nolon turned to look into Misty's black eyes and her arms mutated before him. Her arms became tentacles in a slow-motion hallucination and more grew from her back like those statues of Shiva, the four-armed Indian devil. Misty's six tentacle-arms wrapped around Nolon's whole body, he was bound to her in a firm, snake-like constriction, any thought of escape was foolish.

"What the hell is this? What happened to you?"

"This is my true self, Preacher," Misty's voice was in his head now. "I am the next stage of humanity. We are the next stage, if you will join us."

"Yes, child, he will join us," Axle said. "You see, Preacher, Misty is from my body. I mated with our friends here. We are building a new power. She is the Eve in this re-genesis of mankind. She is the first woman, the first of her kind, but there is yet to be an Adam. Of course, we need a male so that we might prosper and multiply. Tonight we are going to change that, tonight is a beginning, a new beginning to a wonderful movement which has already started. Are you ready, Preacher?"

Misty's tentacles latched his clothing, tiny tendrils grabbed the fibers, expanding and contracting, tearing and shredding it with hardly any movement whatsoever. Everything he was wearing dissolved under the tentacles and he stood naked in front of them. Nolon looked at the pile of threads and frayed rags at his feet and a new fear rose in him.

"What are y'all doing with me?" Nolon began to sweat, his skin gooseflesh. His southern accent heightened in the panic. "I, I ain't nothing but a no-good crackhead. I ain't nothing to y'all. I ain't nothing no-way."

"You are perfect, Preacher," Misty's soft breath in his ear. "We have been watching you. Physically, you are what we need. You can lead, you can move your congregation. There are important people in your church and you will be their master and savior. You, Preacher, will unveil Jesus' new plan to all of humanity."

Misty's tentacles tightened. Axle rose from her chair. Nolon's chest constricted. He tried to move, to loosen Misty's grip but there was no slack in the tentacles, but neither did she tighten on him. Axle's gaze locked his eyes and the thrumming in his mind resumed. He relaxed a little. Then a little more. He felt stoned, like from a muscle relaxant or a small shot of heroin.

"Don't be afraid," Axle said, her gruff cadence smoothed to a purr. She grabbed his testicles with a warm, soft hand. "We will be here to strengthen you, to support you, and to make sure that God's plan is perfectly executed."

He didn't want to relax, he wanted to fight, he didn't like this, this was not God's plan. He tried to flex his legs to kick free. His mind clenched, willing movement, willing himself far away from this depraved madness. The tones moves through his body and he melted in spite of what he wanted, his muscles became liquid, his bones jelly. All he had any control over was his penis which stared dumbly at the carpet, as limp as the rest of him. When Axle thrust a finger inside of him he had no choice; his body reacted, and, like a puppet, his cock raised. Misty's breath on his neck helped ease things. Axle milked him coolly and dispassionately, as a dairy farmer at a cow's udder. When his seed spilled, Axle collected the fluid in her hands, holding her hands out as though and walked behind Misty.

"You and Misty are going to have a child. We could have done this another way, but I wanted to be a part of the conception." Axle kissed his cheek. "Her pussy don't reproduce, it's like a duck's fake hole, there's an opening in her back."

Misty cooed in his ear, her voice low and breathy, "I feel you inside of me, Preacher. Your seed is planted. Soon, we will have a son."

She released Nolon. His legs gave way and he stumbled forward to the floor. He could see Misty's body morph. Her hips spread, her stomach pushed out. It was like a time-lapse video of what had happened to his wife, those fun photos taken every week at the same place in the house, in front of the china cabinet her mother gave them, to show her stomach poking out further and further.

Those were wholesome days full of laughter, they were thrilled at the prospect of being parents. They'd bickered and quibbled over names, he recalled, playful teasings that left a warm impression even to this day. There was no warmth here, this was as close to laboratory procreation that he could imagine. He wanted to vomit. His seed was spawning a beast with tentacles and black eyes. Not Satan spawn, his own spawn with a woman he thought he could save but who was playing him all along. He'd liked Misty, he wanted to introduce her to Melody so the three of them could... He found his speed and a car key in the rags on the floor. The key shoveled it up his nose, to his brain, and he burst forth into a bright, new, shiny day.

"Preacher, you okay?"

Nolon couldn't speak. He felt ice in his chest, his skin was crawling with the tweakiness in the speed, his stomach lurched. He looked at Axle, his eyeballs bulged and his face froze in a horror-mask.

"There is nothing to be afraid of."

He'd never thought of Axle as the maternal type. She put her arms around him and he felt warm. She whispered in his ear like his mama used to do when he couldn't sleep. She held him and rocked him in her arms, both sitting on the floor. Misty took Axle's seat and her belly continued to grow.

"How will that thing..." Nolon couldn't finish a sentence.

"It comes out where the seed went in, like normal," Axle explained. "The development is much faster, though. You'll have a five-year-old with you in church today. We're naming him after you."

"I think it's soon." Misty slid from the chair and lay down on her side.

"Are they all like that?"

"Your son will be a special boy," Axle said, squeezing his shoulder. "It's hard to say what'll happen. All sortsa shit came up in the lab. He'll be healthy, smart, and strong, we know that for sure."

"What about him? Those fucker's ain't right."

The man in the chair turned to face Nolon. His face was pale, impassive, and his black eyes sat softly in his face. Nolon looked into the face and his previous fear and anger dissipated. The thrumming on his spine resumed. A sense of peace and calm came over him, and a healthy glow appeared around the man's head, saint-like, harmless. Nolon took a deep breath and looked back to Axle.

"This is the future of humankind, Preacher," Axle said. "We are God's chosen people, beings, or whatever. The wisemen in the fields saw lights in the sky the night Jesus was born. These men were there, they helped. Those lights were their ships, Preacher. Do you see it?"

"Oh my god."

"Yes, Preacher, it's happening. The lion will lie with the lamb, the wolf with the calf, and," Axle pointed to Misty's still-growing belly, "a child shall lead them."

"You mean?"

"That's what the prophets say, all the signs are there," Axle patted his nappy hair. "But, you must teach him and guide him. You're the one, Nolon. Since your birth you've been special, you know that."

Nolon knew. He had that scarred tree to prove it. He had years of adversity, struggle, and triumph to prove it. He had trudged the road of the spiritual hero, overcoming negativity and ignorance, the temptations of Satan, and the lies of godless, decadent Philistines. He knew he'd been called out west, to Portland, to do good work and he'd always been so certain the knew what that work was. Now he saw that he was wrong, his missionary work with the wretched was only a ruse by God, a test to see if he'd succumb and abandon Him; his work with Melody and the whores was only a step on his path to true destiny. His human mind never could have foreseen such a fate befalling him and now he again marveled in the genius of God's plan.

He wondered when Jesus figured it out that he was the son of God. He was a special boy, intelligent and curious about God, but when was it made apparent to him that he was the Son of God? Nolon thought that maybe now he'd have an opportunity to ask, when he sat with his son on a pearly-white throne next to Jesus. They'd be three black men in a glorious white and gold chamber, sitting on huge chairs, ruling in heaven forever.

"I will teach him, he and I will lead the next wave of humanity," Nolon said. He rose to his knees and went to Misty, he put his hand on her belly and closed his eyes and silenced himself to pray.

"The Lord has called us, my unborn son. He has called us to lead his people to a better tomorrow, he has chosen us by some unknown, holy alchemy, to enlighten and teach those who might react in fear. I have reacted in fear and anger, and I suspect many more will do the same in the days and months to come. But, we will be strong, son, and we will make them strong so that they might walk with us on the path to a new and brighter tomorrow. We will bring light to the darkness which entraps them, and where they suffer with ignorance we will bring wisdom. The Lord flows through us and his divine truth prevails in times of strife and trouble. Our cause is righteous, my son, and we will rise to meet the challenge. I still have fear of you, son, you are different than me, but I will love you and you will love me. You will show me to not be afraid and I will show you everything about this wretched world, that we might save it." Nolon bowed his head and was silent. His hand vibrated and a tremor moved up his arm; he could feel his son transmitting energy and goodness from the womb to his heart. His chest inflated and tingled. He clenched his eyes shut to contain the overwhelming goodness which fluttered through his body, which he knew could reduce him to a puddle, a blob of happy goo on the floor. He stiffened himself to contain the joy of anticipation, to prepare for the work to come. "In Jesus' name, amen."

Nolon knelt on the floor, his forehead sunk into the carpet and his body vibrated with ecstasy, his muscles jumped in spasms. His mind was reeling in the speed, the lack of sleep, and his final ascendance to glory. He heard Axle and Misty speaking, but their words were lost on him; the man walked past him and out of the room. Then there was a scream. Nolon lifted his head.

Misty had reclined her chair and was lying on her side. Axle was stroking her forehead and rubbing her belly. This was it. Nolon sat in excitement, he was about to become a father to the most special child the earth had ever known. His head spun. How long ago had Axle taken his seed? He stared at Misty and the clarity came to him. Hardly an hour had passed, maybe two. The sermon was coming fast, he'd have to start thinking about cleaning himself, putting on fresh clothes, combing his nappy crackhead hair.

Nolon's anxiety was overwhelming. Misty started moans of pain as the inhuman birthing began. He stood and saw the opening in her back, the organ pulsed with her moans and it dilated much like his wife had dilated. He paced back and forth, unable to take his eyes from her organ. Sweat poured from his brow. Axle opened a closet and set out towels for the procedure.

"Y'all got any whisky?"

"Typical male," Axle said. "Some will be down soon. You like Dewar's, right?"

"Neat."

Time ticked slow in Nolon's mind. He stared at Misty's back and listened to her rhythmic, breathy moans. He'd seen some messed up stuff in his life, but this beat all, this made all the disturbed crackhouse sex acts, the violence of the streets, even the glory and horror of his hallucinations seem paltry and pedestrian. This was a move past humanity, to a new, higher form of person. He'd only known the lowest forms. He had been so happy doing mission work amongst the dregs of humanity. Sometimes they would listen to him and he could preach the gospel truth and he thinks he saved few. They disappeared and never were heard from again.

Perhaps their bodies were in the landfill or maybe they returned to their mama, got themselves into rehab or church or bare-knuckled detox and rebuilt themselves on their own terms. He couldn't tell, that was for the Lord to know, his part was to show the way, to preach gospel truth and to show the love of the Lord.

A man appeared at his side with a bottle of whisky and a heavy highball glass. He also had a robe for him, a long black robe like Axle's. The air was warm and Nolon was so high that he'd never feel a chill anyway. The robe appealed to his sense of modesty and he thanked the man, who said nothing.

"Hallelujah!" Nolon took the bottle, cracked the seal, clenched the neck with his fist, and poured a drink; his jittery hands spilled the booze and he concentrated and tried to pour it steady. He kicked the cap under a chair and the whisky went down smooth, like sweet milk, as his Daddy always used to say. His Daddy always drank Dewar's if he'd been winning at dice or cards, or if he'd been able to pick a few winning teams. The family's main source of income was often High School football, his father knew how to get to players. He'd ply them with booze and women so that they'd throw a game or two. He had a few coaches wrapped around his finger. Teens would do it with the fattest redneck in town for a few bucks and Mr. Tankersley was enough of a photographer to keep focus before getting totally shitfaced. It was a living. Things were going well until one night when he opened his mouth in a poker game. He'd rigged the state championships and won several thousand dollars. He'd bought a bottle of whisky and got just drunk and proud enough to talk about it. The police found his car next to a swamp and his blood was on the seat; his body was never found, Nolon figured it was eaten by an alligator. He filled the glass halfway and raised it above his head. He looked into the brow liquor swirling in the light, the lead crystal weighed heavy in his hand, and prisms shot through the design some genius glass blower had etched into it. He was silent, but his heart was heavy. Not even Axle's speed could harden the feelings he felt in that moment. He could barely remember his father's face, but he would never forget his Daddy's chair that sat in the corner of their three-room house. He held that image of that chair in his heart and he made a toast:

Here's to you Daddy, I'm drinking your whisky, like you always said I should. You'd be proud Daddy, your boy done good. I may have been a sorry ass son when I was young, I may have been soft and bookish and talked bad about your drinking and gambling, but tonight I'm fathering the future of the whole world. I wish you could have lived long enough to see it. I know your street smarts and your spirit have been with me, keeping me safe from danger, and even moving me towards the Lord, though in ways I doubt you'd recognize. But it don't matter, because I love you. You could bet on me, Daddy, you'd win every time. Here's to you, Daddy, I miss you every day. Nolon drained the glass in a single slug.

Misty screamed.

Nolon saw his son's head first. It was full of curly hair, smeared with amniotic juice, his eyes remained closed under the goo. Axle jumped in to deliver the child, its tentacle arms waved in the air, its lungs expanded and filled the air with the shriek of life's first trauma. She handed the child to Misty, who licked the child's face clean and offered him her breast, which he took with gusto. That's my boy, Nolon thought, a big man's appetite. He was so happy; he poured more whisky in his glass and drank it.

"Can I hold him?"

"Let him feed," Misty ran a finger on the child's head and licked it clean. "He's hungry."

Nolon paced. He had to think of a sermon. He was still a preacher and a dutiful servant. God's people had been persecuted by the Philistines for too long, he'd say, false prophets and pagan ideas had dominated the country for too long. Now heaven was sending down a holy army to help the deliver the righteous from suffering. Spiritual slavery would end soon, freedom would come at the hand of newcomers who might be frightening but who would bring the next wave of existence. Yes, spiritual slavery, that was the key, that was IT.

"Got something to write on in this place?"

Axle nodded, "Sit tight."

A man entered the room with a pen and a pad of paper.

"How the fuck did you do that?"

"You'll be able to, too," Axle said. "The drug does

it, it opens up your mind in new ways. Have you seen visions?"

"Yeah."

"Not like regular speed, is it?"

"Hell no."

"Give it a few weeks," Axle said. "We have you pegged for a quick adopter like I was. A whole new world is opening up, Nolon. Welcome."

Nolon wrote like a madman, the sermon flowed from his mind to his hand as though it was being dictated by the Lord himself. The words were making themselves, he thought, he only had images and vague notions of what he wanted to say but the prose was the best he'd ever managed. He would make women cry and the men would be filled with a pride from God. The sermon spoke of humanity's potential and how the Philistines amongst us had been holding back God's holy plan. How he had sent emissaries to lead the way, men whose job it was to lift us all up to a new future.

"Do you want to hold your son before he's too big to be held?" Misty held out the child for Nolon, who went cold.

"You sure?"

"It's human custom, right?" Misty's eyes were warming him. "Everyone here held me when Axle gave birth. We have the same custom, in our own way."

Nolon held out his arms and took the child. It squirmed in his arms, its tentacles wiggled and grabbed his arm. Nolon captured his son's eye and the two looked into each other. Nolon felt a deep-down warming at the base of his spine, his stomach relaxed knots he didn't know he had. His son was beautiful, a perfect bouncing boy even with the arms and black eyes. A father's joy knows no boundaries, he thought, it's as limitless as God, it's the Lord's perfect gift, an inner source of wealth and strength. That his son wasn't human was irrelevant. His human children weren't perfect, either, and he was never an ideal son. He wasn't what his father wanted and he knew that. It was the way of the world, that was in the Lord's plan; he still loved his father and his father had loved hie; he would love this boy forever the same as a human, god-fearing child.

"My beautiful baby boy," Nolon said to a smiling baby face. "You and I will have some marvelous adventures as you grow up, or when you've grown, which looks like will be sometime tomorrow. We have important work to do and I hope I can lead you right. My daddy didn't do me so good, and so far I've screwed up my other children pretty bad. I'll work to correct the mistakes. You are from my real life, though. I was only playing a false role before, trying to play the role of domestic daddy, the good preacher. I mean, I am all that, but I have a larger mission and that mission has led me directly here, to you. It's God's plan, my son, it's been written in the fabric of the universe that we were to be together and to lead the ignorant to a new day. We are history, son. We are divine and blessed."

Nolon kissed his son's forehead and walked around the room. He took each step with thought and care, his heel sunk into the shag and the rest of his foot rolled to flat. He heard nothing but his breath mingled with his son's. He rocked the child in his arms and the boy squinted his eyes and gave a baby-sigh. Things were moving so fast, he knew, but it all felt so natural to him as though everything was right on schedule and according to plan. There was no water available, so Nolon walked over to his glass of whisky and anointed the boy's head with the liquor that had fueled two generations of Tankersley men.

"You may be different, boy, but you're a Tankersley as sure as I am."

"Nolon," Axle said. "You have something to do. Snort a bit more if you want, there's plenty."

"What I gotta do?"

Misty took the baby from Nolon. "It's the next part. You're in good hands. It'll help you in church."

Nolon found a mirror with a line of dope cut and waiting for him. He bent to the table and pulled the powder into his nose. His vision was blotted out for a sea of colored pixels and he felt giddy and gooey. His body was hugged by a mass of arms or tentacles. The druggy euphoria blotted all feeling; he could register pleasure when his body rose into the air with his belly to the sky. His head dropped back and his arms fell away, drooping from their sockets. Colors swirled and spun out new shapes and patterns then the field of colored dots returned. It was a magical show to behold. He felt his body moving, carried through space. He might be flying, or maybe the Lord was taking him. In his state of bliss, he didn't care. If this was death, it would be a beautiful end to one hell of a spin on Earth.

The movement stopped. He found himself lying on a bed. Colors swirled; he could make out bodies moving, they were covered in the colors, the whole room washed in a field of tiny pulsing pixels. He was pressed into the mattress, the arms moved all over his body, under the robe. A tentacle penetrated his ass and his vision flashed alarm red. He heard himself scream; he heard music deep in his mind. What the fuck? He tensed his body to rise up and escape, but there was no slack in the binding. The thing wriggled and moved farther up his intestine. He could feel it in his stomach and his entire body felt bruised and violated. In his eyeballs, he felt pressure, his ears couldn't pop, and he was nearly deaf. He wanted to vomit, but there was nothing inside. He never ate, he couldn't eat, food was a distant memory, but all he wanted to do was to vomit a sea of red bile like he did as a child when he angered his mother and she threatened to call his father. A voice spoke in low, dulcet tones deep into the center of his mind: *Nolon, be calm, you are in a safe place. You are with friends. We need to do this. We knew you would never allow this procedure of your own free will. We do apologize. This is for the best. After the process is complete, you will feel different. You will change. Your life will be better, this we know for certain. You will merge with us. Not everyone is as you are, we have experimented with many humans and very few are made like you. You are responding pos-*

itively to the procedure, so we ask you to relax. We are removing the toxins from your body and you will be able to eat again. You will not wish to vomit and your mind will be clear.

A flood of images passed through Nolon's mind. All of the ugliness he'd ever seen before in his life, all the negative feelings, all of the pain of his life flooded forth. His father beating him, the indignity of wanting to be white, all the crack, dead hookers, drug dealers, and scum of society were facing him and laughing. He poured sweat, blind but for the horror his mind was bringing forth. His mother's hard voice, scolding him, pleading with him. His wife. Her hard gaze penetrated and the sobs of his children bruised his heart. It was too much. He squirmed hoping to erase the taunts. The voices in his mind became louder, each face screamed his name and Nolon screamed in return. His eyes streamed tears and his voice frayed.

He talked to the images. He looked at each one and focused on the lines in their face, the scars on their heads. He didn't remember them so scarred and understood that he was now having special insight into their character and he could perceive the pains and injuries they carried with them. He could see the pain each carried, whether inflicted by him or someone else. Great empathy and compassion came over him as he could feel each of his scars, and all the pain he carried, all the anguish from childhood straight through to that very moment.

"I love each of you," his vocal chords felt long and

strong, his chest resonated with a manly voice he had not heard since he found crack, Melody, and the Hotel. "I've hurt many of you and I've not done enough to save others, a failure of my character which only sought to get high and stay high. Living or dead, I love you all. I forgive all of you who may have hurt me and I hope those of you I hurt can some day forgive me. God has a plan for me, I know this. Each one of you has been instrumental in my progress to this state, so know that God has a plan for you which will be revealed when you are ready."

The voices toned down and Nolon's mind became quiet. The faces, too, faded from his mind's eye. Nolon could swear he saw each one soften, close its eyes, and find a shadow of a smile as it dissipated. His body relaxed into deep suppleness and strength. He took a deep inhale and his whole spine popped and adjusted, a flood of energy shot to the top of his head. Weights fell away, burdens he was not aware he held lifted from his body as though inflated with hot air and cut from a tether. He at once felt lightness but also heaviness as his body sank into the mattress in a restful gravity. He hadn't slept in three or four days and the sensation of genuine sleepiness was welcome. The colors behind his eyes scattered to black and Nolon's consciousness slipped away.

A pair of black eyes stared into his, a small boy sat on his chest. His body was limp and embedded in the mattress. The boy was hard-edged and heavy, full of love and excitement for the day. The boy's eyes blinked. He blinked. The boy giggled.

"Get up, Daddy."

"How long," Nolon said, searching for words.

"You slept a few hours," the boy said. "You have to get ready to go to church. I brought you a new suit and you need to shower, you stink."

"Thank you, son," Nolon said. "Err... a lot has happened boy, what is your name?"

"Nolon, the same as you," he said. "Nolon Jr."

"That's right, son. Absolutely right."

Steam filled the shower stall and Nolon could smell himself, the days of not bathing had built a ripe funk on his body. The heat caused him to sweat a bit and the last of the chemicals leeched out through his skin. He stayed in the shower until the chemical odor passed. He hadn't felt so good and real in years, it seemed. His body, his temple, was clean and ready to receive the present moment. His mind was crystal-clear, he could see everything as it was. No more junky "moments of clarity," he would deliver a holy truth which would inspire the world to action. He knew he'd be able to spout a sermon extemporaneously. He'd review his drugged ramblings, but he knew what he needed to say. He was about to save humanity.

He adjusted the water to a near-scalding temperature and he knelt and bowed his head all the way to press on the tile. When he closed his eyes, he saw deep, dark, empty space. Infinity lay behind his eyes and his body was a hollow vessel full of nothingness, ready to accept everythingness. *Dear Lord, send me strength, send me all you got. This humble servant is here for you. I need you more than ever. We will be victorious and the future will be bright. The world faces new challenges and your people will need strength, which I can pass from you straight to them. Heavenly Father, you have given me so much and I am eternally grateful and I am willing to pay whatever price it takes to make you proud. In Jesus' name, amen.*

The suit fit. It had been tailored to his exact measurements. He stretched his arm out and it barely uncovered his wrist, it was snug and roomy in the shoulders. It was black with a dark grey tie. It was striking, it was the finest piece of clothing he'd ever worn and it felt like a glove on his body, elegant and fierce. The shoes were soft Italian leather, his feet floated on clouds. This is the sort of suit a man needs to wear on the most important day of his life, he thought, or for the final voyage to the great beyond. He took a deep breath into lungs that felt fresh and young, his body tingled from the relief the air infused through every cell of his being.

"Daddy looks handsome!"

"Are we going to church as a family?" Misty's body had returned to normal and she was dressed in a plain, beautiful, gingham dress. Axle was transformed in her Sunday pantsuit, and Nolon Jr. looked like a regular little boy. He chafed at a too-tight collar, and played with his clip-on tie. It was a freaky family, but it was a family, Nolon thought.

Nolon drove his new family to the church. His son

had never left the house before and asked a million questions about trees, clouds, and the car. He nearly exploded with laughter when an elk lept onto the road. Misty acted like a wife and held Nolon's hand, squeezing gently as they fielded the boy's questions, elaborating on each other's knowledge of the natural world, each bowing to the other's interruption, each respectful and at ease. This moment is what family is. He squeezed Misty's hand and their bond solidified to a diamond hardness and a foggy morning's ease and softness. The road was empty and lit by gauzy white light filtering through low grey clouds.

Nolon pulled into his parking spot. He took a moment to look at the sign, *Reserved for the Reverend,* and he realized how much he'd overlooked and had taken for granted. He had been robbing his flock more and more each week. The church owed on its mortgage and the roofers still hadn't been paid for patching the hole last summer. Nolon had snorted, smoked, and shot-up every spare bit he could skim from the plates. The church elders were none the wiser. He'd plotted a break-in to steal the sound equipment, which he could easily fence for a few hundred dollars. For some reason they trusted him, even when he knew he reeked of marijuana, booze, and dime store perfume. He'd conned them into believing that his wife had turned into a lesbian and had run off to join a commune, stealing his children and breaking his heart. They still reserved a spot for him, and they hung on every word he said. He was like a god to them, incapable of doing wrong. Now he could set things right and make amends. He would save them all. Nolon took a deep breath to absorb this revelation and to move him through the next moment; he opened the car door.

The family piled out and followed him to his office. There was a backlog of voicemails and his secretary had pasted his monitor with notes, his chair was stacked with faxes and invoice. He put the stack on the floor and sank into his glove-leather chair. It all seemed so shallow and petty, minor details of a minor life. Everything was about to change.

"Hey, everybody, I need a little time to get my thoughts together, okay?"

"You feel good about this. Right, Preacher?" Misty took his hand and sat on his lap. "I'll suck your cock when you're done." Her voice was low and smooth in his ear.

"Mom, can I explore?"

"Here, use this, there's a café a block down," Nolon handed over a banking card. "Come back in an hour when people will begin showing up."

Nolon found himself alone in his office. He had a wall full of books that were coated in dust. He'd only read a few of them, the ones he'd needed to get through his schooling. Once he'd graduated, he'd been too arrogant for books and preferred using that time for other things. All the theology in the world couldn't possibly have predicted this situation, he thought. The prophets had missed this event when they searched the stars. No psychics had sounded an alarm. Momentous change was rising. No one saw it coming.

Nolon pulled a notebook from his closet of supplies. He sat down and wrote out the events of the past day: the strip club, the hotel, LaMore's house, the birth of his son, as much as he could recall from the drugged haze he'd been in. It helped to put things into context, he thought. His mind could see each part woven into the next. They know me better than I know myself, he laughed at himself and the foolishness of his once drug-addled mind. But, just as the prophets hadn't foreseen this, just as I could not understand the signs around me, no one can predict the volatility of the future. It's important to be prepared.

Nolon reached in the bottom drawer of the desk and pulled out a metal lockbox. He still had the key, thank God. Inside was his daddy's four-shot .45 pistol, and a box of ammunition. There would be those who would want to stop him, who wouldn't understand. He understood that truth was a bitter pill for the wicked and ignorant. He might need to protect himself. His sermon was going to rattle cages both in the congregation and throughout the world. He ran a cloth through the gun's barrels and loaded bullets into the chambers. The gun was small and fit his inside coat pocket with minimal bulk. No one would know. He could drop it after the service, on his way to greet parishioners exiting the church.

Nolon sat in silence, his mind empty, a blank slate. The emptiness absorbed and dissolved all of his bodily sensations and thoughts into a pure consciousness that was unfettered by the usual chatter that usually kept him company. An occasional thought arose, passed, and did not linger. He thought of his wife and didn't bury himself in a flood of self-pity or rage at her for pushing him to… whatever he used to blame her for. He felt totally at ease in his favorite chair on a beautiful Portland morning. Even if it was 40°, the rain kept the world green, the streams full of fresh water for fish, and the endless shades of grey were cloudy things of beauty. His mind found silence; he watched clouds morph on their slide across the sky. Stoic stillness froze the air until he parishioners began to fill the parking lot. The show was about to begin. He felt a twinge of anxiety. This was the first time he'd deliver a sober sermon in years. He wouldn't even take a drink of whisky, as he'd done since taking over the church. Last week, he drank a fifth of the stuff to maintain an even keel long enough to deliver a sermon, shake a few hands, and get back to his hotel room.

A knock at the door, "Reverend Tankersley? You in there?"

"Yes, c'mon in, Deborah."

The door opened by increments and Deborah, an associate pastor, peeked around the door. "It's not locked. Is there anything going on?"

"Not at all," Nolon said, "What's on your mind?"

"I didn't see you arrive." She stood straight, Deborah was statuesque and beautiful. "Good to see you, Nolon."

"Good to be seen, my father always said."

"Your sermon ready?"

"I know what I'm going to say."

"You know, last week you only managed fifteen minutes."

"I didn't have much to say." Nolon's stomach burned. "This week, the spirit is with me."

"You look better." Deborah remained standing, she narrowed her eyes and walked over to him. "You look showered. Your hair has been combed."

"It's true that I've had some stress and confusion since my wife left me, but I have found a new home in the Lord, he has shown me a new way. I am following Him as though for the first time."

"New suit?"

"Expertly tailored," Nolon said. "Do you like it?"

"We estimate the church has lost fifty thousand dollars," Deborah said. "Mr. Meyer, the accountant, said he suspects more is missing and he's working on assessing exactly how much."

"Oh no!" Nolon couldn't come clean yet, he didn't have the money, too much was riding on this very moment. "Any idea how the money was lost?"

"Stolen," Deborah said. "From what Meyer says, either an elder or a clergy has walked off with it. The investigation is continuing. So, if you have any information that can help us, we'd appreciate it."

"We'll get to the bottom of this, Deb," Nolon said. "Thanks for letting me know. After the service, I'd like to meet with this accountant. I'm certain the money will resurface, who would rob a church? This is the most sermon I will ever deliver."

"I'm looking forward to it," Deborah closed the door behind her.

The familiar junkie-on-the-run panic chilled his heart, he felt like a rabbit cornered by a snake. He liked it. That was living. How did they catch him? He'd been so careful, skimming the cash before it was counted. Or, maybe that had already been counted. It was so hard to sort through the addled memories of a strung-out speed-freak. But, he'd been doing it for so long, why did they have to catch on now? The new transition didn't need any complications, it was going to be hard enough to convince people, to keep them from straying and sticking to the plan, God's plan. He could not let this petty crap stand in his way. The mission became all the more important when put in perspective against this petty larceny.

The pews were three-quarters full when Nolon took the pulpit. Deborah took care of the preliminaries: the baptisms, the introductory scripture readings, the rote parts of liturgy which Nolon had lost interest in as soon as he became the head preacher. When he'd started smoking crack and doing his mission work, children scared him and he refused to do baptisms, fearing that he'd drop the child or infect them in his junkie arms. Parents had implored him to baptize their child into the church, but he demurred, insisting that Deborah had a better way with children, that babies always screamed in his arms, which they did when he was strung out.

"Good morning." He felt his mouth contorting to a smile. He felt the smile. He hadn't smiled in a long time and each micro-muscle sparkled with joy that rose like an ocean wave. "I, uh, I am so pleased to see you all here today on this glorious Sunday. It occurs to me that this rain is liquid sunshine, God's blessing to us. The rain keeps our grass green and alive, and our roses love it, too." The feeling of elation was so extreme, he felt as though he was filled with some holy laughing gas, helium maybe. He could feel a rose blooming in his heart, red and luscious, with thorns that sent prickles of delight through his nervous system. He had to resist the urge to guffaw from the spiritual tickle. He contained the high just the same as he stifled the chemical mania from a blast of speed or crack-rock.

He looked out to the congregation and saw Misty, Axle, and his son. There were several of the men in dark suits scattered through the audience as well. Misty beamed up at him and his son gave a shy, five-year-old wave. This was it, this was the true test. The big sell. He inhaled and filled himself with the sweet air of the church. He stared at his son and thought to himself, *this is for you, boy.*

"My fellow humans. Here we are, in the Lord's house, secure in ourselves. No matter what we have going on outside of these walls, in our homes and in our careers, right now we know that the Lord has us in his hands, supporting us on these pews, holding us close to our loved ones, to old friends and to the strangers who will be our friends if we let them. Because we know that if a person is here, they are probably here for the same reason that we are. We are all seeking the Lord and Jesus' love. We all wish to be bathed in the holy light spoken of so eloquently in our literature. Some of us are desperate seekers, others find the Light. Yet, we are all on the same path, trudging forward, working towards a brighter tomorrow. The word of God binds us today, and, truly, every single day that we walk on this planet. Rain or shine, the light is there growing a green grass on the ground and a flaming rose in our hearts." He hadn't felt so inspired since he was a young man in his first year at the church.

"And yet, there are those, right here in this world, who do not walk the path of the righteous. Modern-day Philistines, foreigners to our way of life, who have lost the way and who wish to steer us in a wrong, evil direction, away from the light and toward the path of lies and deceit. They tell us that homosexuality is permissible. They twist God's holy word to suit their selfish, secular goals. They won't let your children pray to God in schools, where our kids need the strength that comes from faith and belief in Jesus. They take Christ out of Christmas, turning our holy day into a secular free-for-all which is more about the shopping mall than the birth of the Son of God. They will even take God out of your very home if you let them. These people have lost the light, they live in ignorance and their minds are corrupted by Satan's corrupting influence. They will enslave us all if we let them, enslave us in a world so far from the spirit that there may seem to be no hope of return. We wish to resist them and the distractions they put in our path.

"There are so many of them. They are huge. They dominate the television, radio, the computer networks. Hollywood is overrun with heathens who have no sense of Christian decency or morality. Their technology and smarts and savvy deceptions are overwhelming to us at times. It as though God has forsaken us before these monsters, these seeming giants." Nolon paused, took a sip of water from the pitcher left for him. He wanted the congregation to sit with this disturbing, troubling predicament. He scanned the crowd, the teeming humanity. His church attracted black and white, Asian and African. All of humanity is out here, listening, he thought. The words I say here are possibly repeated in tens or possibly hundreds of languages to all corners of the globe. This is where it starts. He started to choke on the water, but took another sip to soothe his throat.

"Excuse me.

"But, be with me people. Be with me and know that there is a way out and we can overcome adversity. Just as in the Bible, when David was faced with the Philistine, Goliath, we will be able to triumph. David took a single stone from his pouch and he put it in his sling, and he hit Goliath's forehead and brought him down. David was no warrior, either. He was a boy." Nolon looked down to his son, who beamed back at him. "Goliath was a large man who had been a warrior all his life. Goliath had age and experience on his side, not to mention size and strength. This was surely a one-sided battle with a clear victor – the Philistine. How many of us would have backed David in a fight like this? Yet David had his faith in the Lord and that was all. That was all he needed. Goliath had all the weapons of war, shields and swords. David had only a boy's sling and stone. So, with his faith and his meager weapon, David launched his stone with confidence and focus and he buried the rock in the Philistine's head and brought him to the ground." Nolon poked his index finger to his forehead to illustrate the rock's target. Misty, his son, and Axle were rapt. He could see that they were hanging on his every word. The inner thrumming began, soothing and strengthening him. He pressed his fingernail into flesh, feeling the sting, the discomfort fought the inner lightness he felt, it grounded him to a hard truth he'd been denying. The boy was only born a few hours ago and here he has tentacles, is talking and acting like a little boy. The natural order says he should be wrapped in a blanket, suckling his mother's breast. His stomach knotted. He pulled his fingernail out of his flesh, aware he'd left a half-moon mark in the center of his forehead. He was waking up, every moment a new revelation brought by new sobriety and the truth of his life. He looked at the men in suits who were scattered around the room. There are too many, he thought, too fucking many.

"And yet, as we look around our society, and the world, we should try to be as Jesus. There are those who would attack us and when we are in such a heated moment, when survival is on the line, we must repel them with our sling and stone. But there are also those to whom we can reach out. The depraved and the sick need our help and guidance. From the junkie whore on 82nd Avenue to the atheist hipster in our neighborhood café, we can help them and bring them into the light of the Lord. If we talk to them, we may find more commonalities than differences. It is possible to find simple, authentic humanity which always overcomes temporary, worldly differences." Nolon took a deep breath and held it. For all the drug-addled preparation he'd done, he was out of words, or his words no longer sufficed. He had more to say, though. The truth that was wriggling in his mind could no longer be contained. The newfound clarity could not contain his treachery without extreme discomfort. He was feeling this discomfort grow and build within him. He inhaled more into his taut lungs. He released the air in a deep sigh which echoed through the sanctuary.

"This leads me to a confession of my own. For quite some time now, and I'm not sure exactly when it started, I have been less than perfect. I have been downright decrepit. I have lain with whores, I have taken drugs, and I have stolen. I have stolen from you all. A hundred here or there to start, then more, and yet even more later. My associate, Deborah, let me know exactly how much this morning. I will repay it all to you, for you have trusted me and I took advantage of that trust. I was deluding myself that I used the money to help save the wretched among us, but I was only using the money to get high. I do think I helped a few, possibly, for the Lord is always with me, if not in my true heart, then at least in my mind and I can share that knowledge with anyone. This does not condone my actions, which I know were wrong. I will say that I stand here before you a sober and clean man. I underwent a cleansing ritual this morning and for that I am extremely grateful. I see with clarity now. My humanity is returned and I must stand and tell you all that there is a true problem brewing in our world. Living among us, there are those who are not human, creatures who wish to do us harm and to replace humanity with their own kind, and to create hybrids with our species." A sharp pain stabbed his mind, every nerve in his body felt as though it were on fire and he screamed. He remembered his daddy's voice telling him to not be such a sorry-ass, to tough it out. He knew he had to buck-up and take this pain like a man. So he did. "My dear, dear congregation. Please look around you, here, there are strangers with us who seek our destruction." His voice was shaking and wavering like a nervous schoolboy, but he soldiered on. He put his hand on the gun. He knew he couldn't take them all out. "I pray you will forgive me."

Nolon shot his son and Misty in the head. As the second bullet met its target, the pain he felt increased 100-fold and he collapsed to the ground, writhing and screaming. He looked to the ceiling, he heard the commotion, the screams and the pleas for someone to call 9-11. He heard footsteps coming his way and he didn't know who it was, but he could not go on any longer. In a motion, he raised the gun,

> his head,
> the trigger,
> the bullet.

Mercy

Winter will not end. It's 40° in June. Rain falls on the hunched shoulders of peasants waiting for a scrap of bread. I don't need the rations, I made allowances before the invasion made itself known. I can take care of myself. My house is self-sufficient, I am a survivor. I'm autonomous in a sea of sheep.

I need to collect what they hand out, I'm grouped with the parasite class. If I don't scan my subderm a few times a week, they will raid my house and take me in for questioning. When they don't find me at the address I registered with them, a whole series of deceptions will unravel, and five years worth of resistance work would go down the drain. This indignity is part of the trade-off. If I can, I sneak my portion into the basket of a less-fortunate soul. They could be jailed for exceeding the ration, or killed by a mob for the extra loaves. With luck, they will have extra food to eat or to share with those close to them.

Two boys watch assassin vids when the rain ebbs. The 'net is full of video mash-ups, silent except for electronic thumping rhythms that rattle the cellphone's speakers; one murder fades into the next and the boys laugh and cheer the best ones. The scenes are short – a bullet shatters a car windshield and it careens through traffic, a swerving free radical transforms a full freeway of cars into a tangle of metal and fire. The Los Angeles vids are best for a pile-up, the extended carnage has been sped up for comic effect.

Some are shot on remote highways along mountain cliffs or on roads cut through forest. The scenes are edited in slow-motion: a single car drives a drizzled road, shards of windshield scatter, the vehicle careens from an arrow-straight trajectory and moves with singular intention off of a cliff to the ocean below, or into a grove of trees. If you're lucky, it smashes an evergreen or a rocky shore and explodes on contact. Some creep to a halt on an empty road and the shooter pelts it with round after round, puncturing the tires, perforating the hood, and piercing the gas tank, causing a climactic explosion. Prima Donna shit, if you ask me.

I peek over the boys' shoulders and see that they're watching a mash-up of the rarest footage: videos thought to be shot by the shooter himself or an accomplice now edited together with an electronic soundtrack. These are of single people, walking, minding their own business in a crowd or strolling alone, suddenly brought to screaming life and then death by a single bullet – two if the first missed its mark. Mainstream viewers prefer explosions and pile-ups, but a special sort of *aficionado* appreciates the artistry and existential poignancy of a human head evaporating to bloody mist in a crowded carnival midway.

There are so many shooters nowadays that I can't

tell which is my work and which is a copycat. My vids are probably buried in the archives of the 'net by now. I kept a reel of my greatest jobs just in case I want to get back in the game, in case I can steady my old hands to the rocks they were. I've gone weak and trembly.

I was one of the first, maybe the third, shooter to start taking people out in a clean, calculated manner. No flamboyant massacre escapades. I ain't nobody's martyr. I have no desire to go down in a hail of bullets, much less a cowardly suicide after a dishonorable shoot-em-up in a mall or schoolyard. At first it was a statement, a youthful act of political violence. I'm not even sure what my statement was, but it had something to do with conformity and the deadly illusion of safety. I was doing a lot of white powder and reading Nietzsche back then. I was into that Will to Power jazz, misanthropy jacked on speeded-out lightning. When I softened and the demands of society came to bear, it became a job.

My clients were people who'd found themselves strangled with debts that threatened to cripple their families. Most were sick and the hospitals were starting to send around collectors for any medical equipment or to bully their children. So, they'd separate legal ties to their family and I'd shoot them in the head on I-5 or a crowded city street, jogging through a the forest, or wherever they chose. I took my fee in the form of jewelry and whatever cash they had. My bloody graffiti redeemed by economic necessity; I made money in the meantime. I didn't make as much as a corporate assassin, those guys have limos and mansions, but I made enough. One client paid me so well that I was able to buy his country house in the post-mortem foreclosure. I stayed there and I haven't left.

The bread line stretches around the block. We move a few feet an hour, we wear shoes worn to thread, patched with cardboard. The sidewalk is littered with broken glass pipes, remnants of junkies smoking that white crap, leaving no place to sit. Recruiters from the Corporation speed up to the corner and healthy men jump out in military precision, black boots polished and gleaming. They post flyers advertising jobs: *As seen on Oprah; The world's largest employer; Benefits; Competitive pay*; *Opportunities*. There are numbers to call if you prefer a job in administration, manufacturing, or skilled trades. We all have phones; we could all call and put an end to waiting in line for bread, but only a few do. No one hears from those people again. Each day the line grows longer.

"Will you go?" A pregnant woman with hollow eyes grabs my arm with a desperate claw.

"You go ahead, take my place in line." It's a simple gesture. It's all I got. She'll get a hunk of bread five minutes before I do.

"My daddy went." She looks me in the eyes. "Will he come back?"

"Dunno, lady," I say. "I keep to myself."

"He was supposed to send money for food. I wanted to eat like the Freshies, the Goodones. My baby…"

"When did he leave?"

"Before I was born."

Her baby-belly sticks out like a basketball on a skeleton frame. Her voice is a raspy whisper. She's weak and bread is not the solution.

"My baby don't kick any more."

I used to put bullets in bodies like hers. I placed them with precision. I lined up shots with care to ensure that I hit the mark. If I wasn't certain I'd hit the head, I always nailed the chest. The bullets delivered such a force of velocity that nobody escaped destruction. I atomized hearts from 200 yards. I ended the misery of hundreds. I saved their families the torture of prolonged suffering and indebtedness to hospitals and banks.

If I committed any crime, it was theft. I stole death-profit from the fat fingers of usurious men unworthy of their hand-tooled leather shoes. That's what they'd prosecute me for. The charges might read otherwise, but the unspoken crime, the depletion of profit and reduction of control, were my most subversive sins.

I look at her vacant eyes; I imagine a little laser dot in the center of her forehead. I see the explosion of brain and blood from the back of her skull. It would be over faster than a snap of two fingers. She would hardly feel a thing. Lights out. Her baby doesn't have a name yet. The suffering of two ameliorated with a slug of lead. But, I'm too close and that sort of killing is still frowned upon. Even though I was a celebrity in my time, a pop-culture icon that corporations used in secret subterranean marketing campaigns, they'd hang me in Pioneer Square along with drug dealers, pickpockets, and renegade financiers.

"I'm Brady."

"Maya."

We wait. Hours pass. One of the boys dares the other to call for a job and the boy dials the phone. He talks but I can't hear. The conversation is not long and in a few minutes a black van shows up. The military men jump out, identify the boy, and escort him away. He looks bewildered, scared. His friend laughs and yells, *send me a text from the other side*. I turn to the kid. I wanna tell him to forget it. I wanna tell him to run. The men from the van return and surround the boy. They shift positions in rapid succession, hammering the kid with questions, they laugh with him. There's a rising energy, a low chant starts. The kid is laughing with them and the din erupts to a rousing *YEAH*! The men walk the second boy back to the van, they have their arms around his shoulders like old friends. The side door slides to a clanging shut and the entourage disappears as quickly as it arrived.

The line moves forward a few feet. The woman begins to sway.

"I'm dizzy."

"Are you okay?"

"Where's Teague? Where's my daddy?" She starts to sway, her legs are locked.

"Don't know any Teague."

She starts to crumple and I slide my arms under hers, a supported collapse. She won't make it much longer. What I wouldn't give to be on a rooftop with my goddamn rifle and a .50 caliber round in the chamber. With a little distance, I could blow her brains all over this sidewalk. This bitch is going to fuck up my whole world.

I pick her up and carry her. I parked my truck blocks away in a patrolled neighborhood, where the cars aren't burned shells or converted into shelters or brothels. She's light and I'm strong so the mile or so is not much trouble. I've managed to keep in shape with a regular yoga practice, weights, and long runs in the woods. She murmurs a dreamy conversation. Her eyelids shut out the desperation; her brow releases its furrow.

I recline the front seat and lie her down, strapping her with the seatbelt. She moans and adjusts. She doesn't stir when the diesel engine rattles to life or my stereo blasts. I reckon sleep this deep will heal her and the baby. I know shit about babies, but I know a little about the need for sleep after a wound. Starving half to death counts as a wound, if you ask me.

The road is empty. No one can afford fuel. Everyone is trapped at home. Goddamn sheeple pinned and controlled by the illusion of economics. They need something to believe, so they believe what they are told. This is what made the takeover so easy. Bullets are messy, minds can be captured with a television and the right level of fear. I make my own fuel. I'd be put in jail if I were found out, but so far I've managed to avoid detection. I run on biodiesel I brew from old cooking oil, yard waste, or whatever I can find. The old days of straight french-fry grease are gone. They'd smell me in a second, and I'd be arrested under the Petroleum Laws. It's not worth their while to check on waste oil from Hung Low, my local Chinese restaurant, so what was once heartburn waiting to happen is now pushing me down the road in a half-ton pickup.

We cruise the curvy, rain-slicked road along the Columbia River. The lazy snake is a timeless reminder of nature's patient power. We, too, may be able to survive this. Or maybe the woman's baby will see a new era in human existence, or the baby's great-grandchildren, if an asteroid doesn't crash through the stratosphere and destroy all we know and all the shadows we've left. I gotta hope there's an end to this somewhere. I know these fuckers are looking to use us as food when the final phase of colonization begins, but I can't say when it'll happen or if we'll be able to mount a strong enough resistance.

People have tried in the past. Mighty uprisings struck hard at hives of Worm-Men, but were sloughed off like dead skin. The police never found evidence and the cases went unsolved. The resistance leaders were wary to share information with authorities, suspecting infiltration. Life in a paranoid world is isolated, full of fear and anger.

She is still sleeping when I lift her out of the truck. I guess it's good that I'm so tall. I lay her on my sofa and pull food out of the refrigerator. I keep a secret garden and an underground greenhouse so I have fresh produce year-around. I've also stockpiled rifles and ammunition to hunt game and I keep a rabbit hutch, but my favorite is fish. The fish stock improves as fewer people populate the Gorge. The Earth is healing as humanity wanes. Nature is breathing a sigh of relief at the ending of an illness that has plagued it for so many years.

The woman begins to stir. I decide to make her juice. I cut vegetables and feed them into the juicer. The wail of the machine brings her to life.

"Don't worry." I hand her a small glass of frothy green liquid.

"Who are you?"

"Leo."

She drinks the juice and her eyes pop open. Her body is probably so starved for nutrition that she's feeling a little high or lightheaded from the sudden influx of vitamins and minerals. She wobbles on her feet. I lead her to the kitchen table. I pour her a glass of water.

"What was in that?" She blinks her eyes and shakes her head.

"Vegetables, good stuff."

"It tastes like ass."

Maya floats around the house like a swollen ghost. She talks when gestures fail. Her arms dangle behind her when she walks. Her voice is full of air, wind spins in the back of her throat and the words are gentle howls.

Her eyes open wide when she speaks and she never blinks. She's spooky, but it's nice to have a woman around again. Her movements are undetectable, but I notice that my dishes are done and the crust on the bathroom sink is gone. My sheets are clean and my bed is made. I'm remembering what it means to have a "woman's touch" around the house.

I had a girlfriend once, Muriel, she was beautiful and strong. She wanted love, but couldn't release the pain that drove her. She's one of LaMore's girls now. I feel a gurgle in my chest every time I think about it.

"Who's the father?"

Her face loses its color. Her huge brown eyes narrow and look at the ground.

"There were too many."

"Customers?"

"Rich boys, Goodones. In the shadows of the church. Laughing. I was walking. Grabbed me, pulled me…" Her eyes darken. I feel a knot in my chest but it's weak. There's a feeling for her, but its buried beneath layers of callous. These days are so horrible.

"I need to find my father." She latches onto my torso and my arms fall over her back.

"Teague?"

"Yes." Tears pour from her eyes." I need him so much. My mother says he was a good man. He was strong and loyal and full of love. He could play music."

"Any idea where he went off to?"

"To work. He saw a show on, *Oprah*, and he left a

few days later," she holds me tighter. "I was conceived the night he left. He never wrote or called. I wrote him letters at Christmas and my birthday. Nothing came back."

She leans into my chest, silent. I put my arms around her body and my shirt soaks through with her tears. Her body shakes a bit but she makes no noise. We stand there for minutes on end. The air of the cabin cools on my face. I inhale and savor the quiet of the moment. Her body has stilled me; my mind is calm. A crow caws.

She screams. She clamps me in a death-grip and screams again.

"What the hell?"

"It's coming."

"What?"

"Baby."

She's clinging to me and her legs are wobbly. I pick her up and carry her to her bed. Fuck. That kid can't be born here. It's registered already.

"Where is it supposed to be born?"

"Portland General."

"Alright, we gotta go."

"No!"

"This house is not registered. We're off the grid. They'll be looking for that kid the second it's born," I say. "Did they 'derm him?"

"Yes."

"They'll be here in a matter of hours, if not minutes."

She starts huffing and puffing. "No. Fucking. Hospital." Her face clamps into a red grimace and she growls through the contraction. "They take the big ones."

"I'll figure something out." I haven't called anyone in the network in years.

◇

"Goddamnit, the fucking thing is chipped." I can't talk long and Rizzo isn't helping any.

He hangs up. One more call.

"Yeah, it's me." Silence.

"You shouldn't be calling here."

"C'mon man, I got a situation."

"Yeah?"

I tell Spiral the deal. Maya screams. The contractions are coming fast.

"Look, this is stupid." Spiral's voice jumps and cracks; he's jacked on that goddamned speed. "You know babies are their favorite, *the tastiest morsels* is what they say. They'll be looking to snatch that thing up for tests or tasting parties."

"Well, look, we can try to save it or I'm left saving my own ass and leaving them to, well, you know."

"How close are you?"

"You know where I live. I can be there in fifteen."

"Goddamn. All I ask is that you bring some of that good bud."

Maya screams at every bump in the road. She pants, her face puffs red, and tears stream down her face. I can feel the waves of pain and struggle; I tell her to breathe. I hand her a bottle of water. She gulps and gasps. She's on her back, knees up in the air. I sense the heat of life coming from between her legs; her body is beginning a metamorphosis from girl to woman, from woman to mother. A squirming fish is inside of her, a human baby ready to emerge, coated in slime, screaming with life.

I see one of their unmanned airships patrolling the sky, a black bird flying low in the gauzy winter sky. They never come out here and I didn't think to scan for him before I left. Fuck. I stare at it, imagining some reptilian octopus asshole on the other end maneuvering the machine by remote. He's watching me on screen, zooming in on the vehicle, searching for the chipped child. My vehicle and chip have no official business out here.

Spiral is splitting logs in the yard when we arrive. He was never able to install a geothermal system like I did. I woulda helped him, but he was just too lazy, or more interested in monitoring the 'net for their activities, storing our databases beneath codes of encryption. He lined the walls of his house with a mixture of mud and metal filings that obscure all messages sent or received from the chips. I'm sure that a drone has picked up the kid's signal. I can only hope we have a few hours to work with. Maya screams a contraction.

"Damn," Spiral says. "She's tight as a wire."

"Just carry me, asshole."

The cabin is crammed with electronics. It's all stacked, shelved, and organized in a way I've never known Spiral to do before. He's pulled out a mattress for Maya and has a pot on the woodstove. Steam rises and dissipates in the dry cabin air. Maybe he finally got laid.

"You got blankets?" Spiral has nothing but metal and wires in this place.

"I don't need blankets, you idiot!"

Maya's hand clamps onto my arm and it pulses in time with her contractions. She damn near cuts off my circulation. It fucking hurts. She huffs and puffs, the muscles in her stomach clench. She finds more strength and my bones are bowing from the pressure. Her face is a crimson grimace and she's spewing a babble of expletives. She huffs and gasps and the contraction ends. She melts. Spiral brings a glass of water and I pour some in her mouth.

Shit. She's still wearing sweatpants soaked through with amniotic fluid. I pull them off, her panties, too. I stop. My breath stalls in my lungs and a warmth rises in my heart. I've never seen a vagina so engorged. It's a red, pulsing, portal of life. That's what it's all about, I reckon. That's what I want to protect. Even though I'll never have children, and women always leave, I'm compelled to protect humanity, to ease suffering and to help it propagate and thrive, despite staggering odds. I'm the under; I'm the loser, fighting for a down-and-out home team that would never put me in to bat.

"Holy shit, look at that," Spiral comes to life. He's jumping all around. "The goddamn head is coming out."

"Put your hand under it, catch it."

"The fuck you talking about?" Spiral is chewing his fist.

"Are you high?"

"So what, man," Spiral says. He pivots on one foot like a restless kid trying to stay on base. "I boiled water, didn't I? I let you fucks in my house to have this goddamn illegal child that could get us all... I don't know... Fucking disappeared to hell."

"Where'd you get it?"

"Where you think? Fucking LaMore. He's got the goods." Spirals eyes glimmer thinking about the white.

"You're a real asshole, you know that?"

"It's cool, man. Fucking chill." Spiral spins himself around. "LaMore don't know dick. I bugged his goddamn crib!" Spiral's laugh stutters and chops.

Maya's vice-grip crunches the bones in my hand. "The goddamn baby, Spiral!"

He crouches between Maya's legs. "The fuck do I do?"

"Catch."

I hold Maya, who is puffing and squeezing. She grimaces, sweat-drenched, beet-red, and beautiful.

"Keep breathing, you're almost there."

"The head is out." Spiral's eyes are bugging out of his head. He remains steady and focused.

The child screams for life, the shock of light and air assaults his little body for the first time. This world won't be new for him, it will simply be the way it is.

For something to be new, there must be an old referent, a story into which fresh information arrives. Spiral cradles the boy in a swaddle of t-shirts and handkerchiefs. He hands the baby to Maya.

"Here ya go, mama." Spiral looks like a goddamn saint handing Maya her child.

"Where's the derm?" I have a razor-knife in my pocket. "Spiral, you know where they put those things?"

"If you take it out, it'll send an alert which they won't ignore. If they can't find it, there'll be hell to pay."

"But, it'll constantly send signals. The fucker is supposed to be in the hospital." Maya is nursing her child.

"We're all three supposed to be disappeared. If we got what's coming to us, I bet we'd all be dead. It's what we live with, isn't it? It's the path of life. Every second is numbered, every free breath is a blessing. Why is the baby any different?"

I cradle Sam. I hold him to my chest. He sleeps most nights, but tonight something has woken him. I rock and sing to him. He's not my flesh and blood, but he is my kid. I am a father. Where I used to dole out kindness with a bullet, now I help with late-night feedings, and diaper changes. I make goddamn funny-faces and cooing noises.

The room is cold. We never did get a summer and now the rain is back. I lay the child on Maya's chest to nurse. I cover them with blankets and take a seat on the easy chair in the corner. When she feeds him, the whole human drama makes sense. It's about comfort, it's about caring for one another, finding shelter from the storms outside. It's about being who were are as animals, as conscious beings.

Maya and I started sharing a bed for warmth. Or, that's what we told each other. It was warm, and it was nice to defrost the ice that had grown around my heart. I still expect to wake up and find her gone, for her to erupt in a rage when I forget to put the toilet seat down. None of these things has happened yet and I'm getting used to the domestic tranquil. I am getting soft.

She hums to the suckling child, whispers half-asleep melodies in time with the tempo of fading drizzle-drops outside. The clouds break and moonlight streams down on them. Mother and child. Here. I am amazed every time a scene like this arises and I find myself dumbstruck. My heart lights up as though charged with electricity, it reacts to the perfection of the moment and there's nothing my mind can do about it except listen to this once-dormant organ is communicating, even if I can't decipher the messages into words. I'm captive to myself, to a part of my being I never knew had any power.

I open the stove and put a log on the dying embers. Geothermal is effective during the day, when solar powers the fan, or when it's a windy night and the turbines spin. It's a still, dark, night so we rely on fire. I hear a rustle outside. Did I see a shadow scurry? I prod the log and blow on the coals, my breath inspires a flame and a renewal of warmth. The log catches. I shove a few twigs under it, the coals blaze orange when I blow on them, and I shut the stove. I squat, absolutely still in the dark. The house is part of me and there is something near. Maybe it's just a deer or a coyote, but I feel it. I peek out the window and gaze over the moonlit lawn and see something disappear into the treeline. It's too dark and too far to tell what. My heart leaps in my chest, but I tell it that it was nothing. An animal, a figment, a mistake of perception. It was nothing.

Sam has finished feeding when I return to the room. I carry him back to his crib and rejoin Maya in the bed. Her body is warm and I wrap around her, melting into the safety we've built. Her hand reaches for me.

On my way to the woodshed, I find footprints in the mud. Human. The treads are deep. I guess he's a big guy and he is wearing brand new boots. No one has new boots anymore. Shit.

I guess I've always known it would come to this. We're trapped by an invisible foe. We could rip out our subderms and run for it, but where would we go? They are multinational, global; their network is light-ning-quick. We'd soon run out of food. If there are oth-ers like me, others who have autonomous dwellings, I don't know about them or if they'd even take on a small family like ours. We all stay off the grid and invisible to all. We're all scattered, out for ourselves. Freedom runs out when you're on your own. The funny thing is that you need the bonds of other people in order to be free.

"What's the matter?" Maya says. I hoped I could keep this from her.

"Someone's been sneaking around."

"You think it's Spiral? maybe he got high and tried to catch us having sex?"

"Spiral don't have new boots, and the way he's been tweaking, he can't weigh more than a buck-forty," she's wringing her hands. "The tracks were deep and distinct."

We go on with our day. We don't mention it again; there's no need to add new layers to the fear and anxiety. Maya spends time with Sam, she reads when he sleeps; I split wood, cook, and harvest food from the basement. The house is operating at supreme efficiency. I figured out how to increase food production and when we we use the rations from town we have a surplus. I give the excess to Spiral, but I doubt if he's eating. All he seems to do is go to town for speed and sit in his house and get high. He's making sculptures out of used circuit boards, wire, and scraps of metal he finds. The pieces are phantasmagoric, created in that peculiar frenzy that only the extremely high and sleep-deprived can attain.

"Yeah man, some shit is about to go down." There is static on the line. Spiral is running one of his contraptions.

"You have no one else left to call, is that it?" Spiral sounds clear and lucid.

"Look, we're in this thing together," I say. "Give me some contacts, we gotta move. Someone is watching the house."

"Not like them to stalk. They don't hesitate."

"What do you say? Know anyone?"

The line goes dead. Silence. My heart sinks. I don't breathe. I'm frozen looking out the window at the field outside, at the tree line where the stalker's tracks led. I draw my focus back to the window, to the framing of the individual panes, to the dust on that wood. The world goes black.

My eyes open. I blink to focus. I'm lying on the floor. I see a glint of metal in a man's hand. It's a knife with a very long blade. Maya is sobbing in soft tones. I hear Sam suckling her breast. I prop up on my arms to sit against the sofa.

"So, captain, looks like this is the end of the road." It's LaMore. You don't have to ever see him to know what he looks like. The scar, the glove, and the 12-inch blade are his trademarks.

"I been watching you out here," he says. "I been busy and I wanted to wait until my little grandson was a little older. Hell, I was gonna wait until he could hold a gun, but I got impatient. All the white I snort tends to fuck with my ability to abide."

"Grandson?"

"Yup. Hell, I even picked out the father. Well, we

had help. It was important to test the DNA and all that shit. My grandson is gonna be a mighty warrior. He will lead us to greater heights."

"I thought my father was a good man," Maya says. She is staring at Sam. Tears stream from her eyes.

"I run a fucking town. I gave you a son. Your worthless ass would have ended up a spinster had I not intervened. So, say 'thank you papa.'"

LaMore points the tip of his knife at Maya and he grins. The look of terror on her face is palpable. My heart sinks. I want to vomit. "Fucking say it," he says. He points the knife at her; metal teeth glimmer through parted lips.

"Thank you papa," Maya says. She bursts into tears.

LaMore crouches down to me. He puts the tip of his blade in the middle of my forehead and presses it to the bone. A trickle of blood runs into my left eye.

"I like killing boys like you," he says. "Boys who used to be tough but got soft. You were a real killer in your day. I watched your career. Hell, I made sure you got the best white there was. You were like a quarterback or a start pitcher to me. I love bringing people down, showing them who really runs this motherfucker.

"But seeing my grandson here did something to me. You took care of him and you didn't have to. You took care of my daughter, too. You remind me of what I was before I changed, so I'm going to do Maya's bidding and I won't make you watch your own dissection. Nor will I do it fast with a bullet. Instead, I'm going to let you go. You'll have no protection from me or anyone. Your buddy Spiral is gone, as is everyone you've ever known. I have their fingers if you would like proof, but I'll spare you.

"You'll be hunted like an animal, but you're smart enough and stupid enough to survive for a while. At least that's what I reckon. You'll be an animal with a target on your head. I don't know which is worse — death now or what you'll eventually find. But, Maya doesn't want me to kill you and my girl gets what she wants."

The blood turns the world of my left eye red. I am woozy and stunned. LaMore leaves the door open, the cold air washes over me. I sit paralyzed and watch Maya walk out of sight. My son is gone forever. The light of the overcast day makes my eyes ache and the air chills me, my nose is cold and damp. I take a deep breath. Breath is all I have left.

A handful of crows land outside on the grass, in my right eye I see their black bodies against the emerald green. They peck for worms or insects. They hop around in their hunt for a meal and then they all go still. It's like the world stops for a second. It's tinted blood-red in one instant, grey-blue the next. The birds bow their heads in unison, as though hearing a far-off menace, then they burst to the sky and fly away.

"Power demands a redress" — Douglas R. Brooks